I0739218

Appease: Princess and the Pea Retold

DEMELZA CARLTON

A tale in the Romance a Medieval Fairy Tale series

Copyright © 2017 Demelza Carlton

Lost Plot Press

ISBN-13: 978-0-9922693-4-0

ISBN-10: 0-9922693-4-2

DEDICATION

This book is for the real Dorota, whose tales of crossing the Baltic Sea are worthy of their own book.

One

To six-year-old Princess Sativa, betrothed seemed like such a strange word. Mother had told Sativa that it was a fancy word that meant promised. She was promised to the prince, and he was promised to her. When she'd asked what kind of promise, her mother had only smiled and said, "The unbreakable sort."

So now Sativa sat in the place of honour in her father's hall, beside her promised, Prince

Reidar. She wasn't sure what she wanted to do with him. Big boys like him usually spent all their time in the practice yard, sparring with swords and shooting arrows into targets. He had a sword strapped to his side, too, like one of her father's knights. It was smaller than their swords, though, for he was only a boy.

It certainly bothered his mother, though. Queen Regina looked like she'd drunk vinegar instead of wine every time he bumped her with his sheathed sword. More than once, Sativa had been forced to smother her laughter, or risk a quelling glance from her own mother.

Sativa yawned, remembering to cover her mouth before her mother saw. She wouldn't have been so excited about attending this feast if she'd known it was so boring. She'd eaten her fill of the food, and she wasn't allowed any wine, so why did she have to keep sitting there? Normally when she'd finished her dinner, she could go play with her little sisters, or the castle kittens, but her mother insisted she must spend the whole dull day with the prince. Her betrothed.

He'd arrived here on his horse yesterday, and he'd scarcely said a word to her since.

She eyed him carefully as he ate another piece of meat. He had a tongue and teeth, same as her, so he should be able to talk. While she watched, she caught him smothering a yawn. He was as bored as she was!

"Do you want to see my horse?" Sativa asked Prince Reidar.

Reidar turned to Regina. "Mother, may I?"

"Kings do not ask permission, they command," came the reply through Regina's gritted teeth. She eyed Sativa with distaste.

Reidar drew himself up. "Mother, I am going with my betrothed to see the horses," he announced grandly.

Regina nodded once.

"Mother," Sativa began.

"You may go. A feasting hall is no place for children, and it grows late," Mother said. She peered fearfully at the hall's high windows, where the afternoon sun slanted in.

Sativa forced a smile. Her mother had been afraid of the dark for as long as she could remember. Not for herself, but for her children. Apparently Sativa's fairy godmother, Dalia, had told her that her daughters would be stolen from her by evil that swooped out of the darkness. Queen Dorota had lived in nightly dread ever since. "Yes, Mother," Sativa said.

Sativa led the way out of the hall, hearing Reidar's heavier footsteps behind her.

"His name is Philip, and he's really only a pony. Father says I may have a proper sized horse when I am bigger." Sativa glanced back over her shoulder. "As big as you, I think."

"When you are my queen, you will need a proper horse to ride. How else will you go hunting?" Reidar said.

"Queens don't hunt, Mother says. Killing is a job for men."

Reidar laughed. "My mother hunts as well as any man, or so my father says. So do many of the ladies at my father's court. They call it sport, pitting oneself against a noble beast, then bringing its carcass home for the victory feast. When you come to my castle, I will make sure you learn to hunt."

Forbidden pleasures and a new horse. Maybe her betrothal wasn't such a bad thing.

"What else do you have in your castle?" Sativa asked. "Will I get to wear beautiful gowns like my mother does?"

"Fit for a queen, I am sure. You shall choose them," Reidar said.

Betrothal sounded better and better.

Sativa led the way out to the fields beside the castle, but there wasn't a horse to be seen. "Where are they?" she asked in dismay. She found a guardsman at the castle gate. "Where are the horses?" she demanded.

"This time of day, the horses are all in their stable, having dinner, young mistress," the guardsman said.

Sativa wasn't supposed to enter the stables, but with her mother and everyone else at the feast, no one but she and Reidar would ever know. "We must speak of this to no one," she said imperiously as she led the way.

know. "We must speak of this to no one," she said imperiously as she led the way.

Two

His mother was wrong, Reidar decided as he followed the little princess. Sativa would make quite a queen one day, if her six-year-old self was any indication. As long as no one did anything to dampen her fire between now and their wedding, which would be at least a decade away. She had her mother's fair colouring, so she'd probably grow up to look like her. Regal and feminine and fiery — everything his kingdom needed in a queen, for if the border wars continued, she would need to rule while he kept the neighbouring armies at bay like his father was doing right now.

She might not hunt yet, but she at least rode. That was good, and she knew her way to the stables well enough. His sisters would not be so sure, leading the way around his father's castle, but the princess of a bigger, more prosperous kingdom like this one, living in a castle surrounded by such a huge town, would need to be more assured than the girls at his father's seaside castle back home.

"This is Philip," Sativa announced, waving at a fat pony that looked very much like a hairy barrel with legs. A hairy barrel that snorted, blowing his mane up off one baleful eye that stared disdainfully at Reidar for a moment before it disappeared beneath the descending mane. "He likes apples." She fetched an armload of fruit from the apple barrel, her shoes scuffing through the straw.

Then her face screwed up, and she sneezed. And sneezed again. Reidar counted seven in all before he began to grow concerned for her health.

By the time the sneezing fit had subsided, her eyes and nose were running and Sativa needed to hold onto a post to stay on her feet.

Reidar's heart sank. Perhaps his mother was right, after all. He'd need a strong queen, not a weak one, and Sativa's health mattered. She wouldn't just have to rule the kingdom in his absence – she'd have to give him an heir or two to ensure the succession, too.

"Are you well?" he asked.

She sniffled loudly and wiped her nose on the back of her hand. Then she seemed to remember herself, and she pulled out a handkerchief to clean herself up in a more ladylike fashion.

"It's the straw," she said thickly. "It makes me sneeze something awful. My father found a physician who had seen something like this before, in a son of some sultan of a desert land far to the south. He called it rose fever, because the prince sneezes at flowers. Me, I sneeze at straw. Not all straw. Just the stuff we have here, which the farmers insist on growing as pasture because it makes our fields the most fertile in the region. Pea straw, they call it. He said I should go to the desert, where it is dry, or by the sea, where it is too salty for such straw to grow."

Reidar couldn't help it. He laughed. "No wonder your parents wanted us to be betrothed. My father's castle is on a cliff overlooking the sea. The salt breeze blows day and night, so that all you can smell is the sea. When you are my queen, I shall build you a tower, and the topmost room shall be your bower, so that you will never need to sneeze at straw again."

"It sounds like heaven," Sativa admitted. "A place with no straw, where I can breathe. Do you truly mean it?"

Reidar pulled a ring off his smallest finger and held it out to Sativa. "Take this as a symbol of my unbreakable promise. I swear that one day, when I am old enough, I will return to save you from this place, and carry you off to my castle to be my queen."

Sativa smiled. "Just like a hero in one of my nurse's fairytales." She slipped the ring onto her finger, and for a moment, the amber caught the sunset light, glinting gold as the silver setting glowed around it. "I will wait for you, my prince," she promised.

Three

Regina found Reidar, as she always did. "So you already know, then," she greeted him.

Reidar traced his finger around the jewels on his father's crown. His crown now. "Yes, I know. Father is dead of his wounds from some skirmish in the border lands, and they are bringing his body home for a proper burial at sea, as befits the King of Viken."

"You will need to find a wife, and have heirs as soon as possible." Regina continued, as though he hadn't spoken.

Reidar rose. "I shall. Have someone summon Rudolf home. He shall be my heir until someone more suitable is born. And send an envoy to Kasmirus, to bring me my bride."

"Rudolf? The boy was sent south for good reason. His claim to the throne is second only to yours, my son. Some might say his claim is stronger, if only because his father was the eldest son. Best to keep him where he is, or he will steal your throne out from under you before your father's ashes are cold." Regina nodded in satisfaction.

But Reidar would not be dissuaded. "You see conspiracies where there are none, Mother. Rudolf will be sent for, because his father is dead, too, and he must swear fealty to me as his new king. If he refuses, then that is something I must deal with. All the more reason to marry."

Regina's eyes blazed. "There are fertile girls aplenty at court. I will see that they are dressed in their best tomorrow, so that you may make your selection."

Reidar shook his head. "A queen must do more than breed. She must rule, and bring alliances and armies when I need them most. You must go to Kasmirus, and bring back my bride."

Regina laughed. "I am too old to travel, my son. Better for me stay here. Besides, I had heard that King Boreslas lost his daughters to a dragon. Your bride is in the belly of the beast, if I am not mistaken."

"That's the tale they tell at the docks, now? Sailors selling stories of dragons eating maidens in foreign lands? Sounds like a fairytale to me, Mother. All the more reason to send an envoy to Boreslas. He owes me a bride, or an answer." He surveyed the sea from the tower windows. He could see to the horizon from up here, though not the land where Sativa lived. If she still lived. "I give you leave to prepare for my father's funeral, and for my coronation. When my bride arrives, you may also plan my wedding. My father trusted you to rule while he was at war, and it was fitting. But now I am king…and I shall do things my way."

All colour drained from Regina's face. Had she truly thought she could control Reidar as she had his father? More fool her.

Reidar ignored her, and summoned a servant. He gave orders for the court to assemble for sad news, for he knew they must be told of his father's death.

For the king was dead. Long live the king.

Four

Princess Sativa played with her amber ring as she waited for her father to notice she'd arrived. For years now, it had been too small to fit on her fingers, so she wore it on a thong around her neck.

Her heart went out to her grey-haired father, for now he looked like an old man.

Her father had aged a lot since the dragon came. First the loss of her mother, then the dragon plaguing the city, and then the final blow of losing her sisters in one fell swoop, just as the seeress had predicted, though Queen Dorota had not lived to see the dragon devour her daughters.

Sativa's sneezing had kept her indoors, away from the parade where her sisters had died that day. It was bittersweet, to know her affliction had saved her from a fiery death. If the dragon had only torched the fields of straw instead, perhaps she would have seen some bright spot in the animal's advent, but no. It stole sheep and maidens, and only burned knights who tried to slay it.

Or it had until last night, when everyone within a hundred miles had learned of the dragon's death. How it had happened, no one knew – not even those watching from the city walls, for there'd been so much fire and smoke no one had been sure the dragon was dead until a man walked through the gates, carrying a maiden, and announced that he'd killed the beast.

And now her father wanted to hold a feast for the man? It was too much. They were still in mourning for her sisters. To host this sort of celebration when…

"Sativa, my dear! How go the preparations? Do you need a new gown to wear?" Her father was so cheerful it could only be a lie.

Yet she forced a smile that matched his. "The castle kitchens are cooking up the feast to end all feasts, they say, they are so happy the dragon is dead. But I thought, so soon after the loss of my sisters…something more sombre might suit…" She caught the look of horror on her father's face and lapsed into silence.

For a moment, she stared into eyes that mirrored hers. All the guilt and devastation at such a tragic loss, the wish that it had been her instead, and the complete and utter despair of having to live knowing the girls were gone, shone through his irises.

"Your sisters would have wanted a celebration. The biggest, grandest feast ever held in our halls to mark the death of that foul beast. They would want it to be remembered.

It is the end of mourning, for today we celebrate a triumph over the devil himself!" Father said fiercely. "You and all the court will wear your brightest raiment. We will commemorate this day! A thousand years from now, they will still talk about how the dragon was slayed!"

Sativa hoped that sometime in the next thousand years, someone found out how the dragon had been slayed. So far, the only part of it they'd found was its head.

"Yes, Father," she said dully. She would do as he asked, because he was the king, and if he gave in to the despair she knew filled his heart, they would all be lost.

Five

"I find that hard to believe, Sir George. You've slayed monsters that were more troublesome than a dragon?" Father asked.

The dragonslayer – a shoemaker, Sativa had been horrified to discover, who her father persisted in addressing as though he was a knight – looked down at his food, abashed. It took him a moment before he managed to say, "Your Majesty, every monster is troublesome. Your dragon is certainly the biggest beast that I've ever faced, but size is not all that matters.

Some of them are so cunning, or there are so many of them, or they are so intent on killing you…why, it's a wonder I'm still alive. There was this pair of unicorns up near your western border…"

Sativa beckoned a server over to refill her cup. She half-listened to the shoemaker's story, which seemed to include pigs, giants and his paragon of a squire, who had saved his bacon more times than he could count. Every time he mentioned his squire, his gaze swept the hall, settling on a table at the back, where the squires sat. Most of them squabbled over the food, focussed only on stuffing their faces with more meat than most of them had seen in months, judging by their ravenous appetites, but there was one on the end, smaller than the rest, who sat aloof from the fighting.

The small squire turned to look at the dais where Sativa sat, and she found herself staring back in the most unladylike way. The squire was no squire at all, but a woman, wearing leather armour that had clearly been made to accommodate her breasts.

She had saved the shoemaker's life?

Surely not. Had she been the maiden the shoemaker carried off the field yesterday? She must have been hurt fighting the dragon, yet she showed no signs of any injury now.

Sativa shivered. Something about the girl's eyes, even across the hall, chilled her very soul.

She began to pay attention to the shoemaker's story in earnest now, eager for details on what this woman had done.

"Truly, I couldn't have killed the dragon without her," the shoemaker concluded.

Father laughed. "You are too modest, Sir George. But the time has come to make you more than that." He rose to his feet, more unsteady than usual. He'd drunk more wine to maintain the cheer he insisted upon for this event.

"My subjects!" the King shouted. "Lords, ladies, knights, men! We are here to celebrate a great victory. Sir George has defeated the dragon that oppressed us for so long." He raised his cup in a toast, then drank. "And he shall be rewarded!"

The crowd cheered and drank with him, but Sativa merely bowed her head. With all eyes on her father, no one would notice that her cup stayed on the table where it belonged.

"Kneel, Sir George!"

The shoemaker stumbled a little and Sativa prayed that he would not embarrass her father by sprawling at his feet. Someone must have heard her prayer, for the shoemaker managed to regain his balance and make his way to her father without any further mishaps.

Now Sativa drank as the shoemaker droned his way through his vows of fealty to her father. Someone must have coached him, she suspected, because he didn't stumble over the words as he presented her father with his sword.

Her father made him more than a knight – when the shoemaker rose, he was a lord.

This seemed to make him even more nervous – it took him a couple of tries to get his sword back into his scabbard, so that when he succeeded, a cheer rose up from the hall for the newly minted lord.

Even Sativa managed a smile at this.

"And as a final reward for his heroism, I have decided to bestow my only remaining daughter, Princess Sativa, on him in marriage this very night. My personal confessor and priest will marry them in the castle chapel after the feast, and if I'm not mistaken, Lord George will have an heir on the way before the night is through!"

Sativa's smile died.

Six

Reidar sent his advisers away for the day, rubbing his temples. Wearing a crown was a heavier burden than he'd thought, even on the days when the gold circlet didn't sit on his head. Keeping the people of the borderlands safe while repelling invaders and dealing with a dozen attempts to steal his crown…and that was just this week.

He was sorely tempted to find some way to let the would-be usurpers wear the crown for a day, so that they might take on the cares that came with it. On the morrow, they could return to their normal lives with no desire to ever wear that treacherous circlet again.

But he couldn't, in conscience, do it. One man with too much power could wreak a lot of havoc in a day.

Or even one woman.

Reidar sighed. "Mother? I sent everyone away so that I might have some peace. Why are you still here?"

She stepped out of the shadows. The Queen Mother should not lurk so, but no one would have been brave enough to say such a thing to Regina. Not even her son.

"I have a matter of great importance to speak to you about. Alone," she said.

Reidar spread his hands wide in invitation. "Very well, Mother. Speak."

She glanced around. "Not here. There is something I must show you first." She beckoned imperiously, and stalked out of his solar.

Sighing, Reidar followed.

She led him to her own apartment. "Now, line up! Let him see you!" she ordered as she went in.

Reidar wanted to turn around and not follow her any more, but as the king, he could hardly admit to being afraid of what he might find in his mother's chambers. So he sighed again and stepped inside.

"Which one do you like best?" Mother demanded.

She'd lined up a bunch of children. Highborn, by the look of them, and all girls, though it was hard to tell at this age. They had no curves to them for they were all too young to be women yet.

"What for?" Reidar asked tiredly. "I don't need a cupbearer. If you want another lady-in-waiting, it would be better for you to make your own choice. I have no idea what to look for in a female companion."

That was a lie, but he managed to utter it with a straight face. He looked for the ship carrying Sativa every morning and every night, but there had been no sign of it yet. Still, he would ascend the tower again tonight, in the hope that he would see it.

"You like them pretty and young, yes? Well, pick which one you want!" Mother said impatiently. "You need an heir!"

The girls giggled at this, and some of them blushed. Maybe some of them were women, though just barely.

"I'm not marrying some girl scarcely out of the nursery so I can get her with child! Mother, I have a bride, who is on her way here now. Send these girls back to their mothers, where they belong. I will sire no bastards on the daughters of my sworn bannermen. There is no honour in such things. Better to hand the kingdom over to one of the usurpers across the border than fail in my duty as king. I promised to protect my people, not seduce their children!" Reidar glared at the girls, who quailed under his gaze. He softened his expression — it wasn't their fault they were here. They were good, obedient daughters who would one day make fine wives for other men of the court. "Girls, go home," he said.

He waited until they were gone before he rounded on his mother. This time, his voice was cold. "Mother, I am betrothed to Princess Sativa, and until I hear word from her father that she is dead, I shall keep my promise. But even were word to arrive at this very moment that she truly is in the belly of this dragon of which you speak, I still would not take a child to be my queen. We may have been children at our betrothal, but more than a dozen years have passed since then. I have no doubt she is a woman grown, and everything I could expect for my queen. She will not break her promise, and I will not dishonour her or myself in breaking mine." He stared at the doorway the girls had run through in their haste to escape. "Would you have my people think me a paedophile?"

She swelled indignantly. "I would have them think you are a king, seeing to his succession."

Reidar sighed. "As a queen yourself, I need

not remind you that these things take time. Nine months, at least, and sometimes longer. How long was it after your marriage that you gave birth to me?" He met her angry gaze for a moment before he turned on his heel and left.

He didn't need to hear her answer. It had been seven years. Seven years of trying, and giving birth to his sisters and all the other children who had not survived long enough to leave their cradle, before he had come along.

If his people had to wait seven years for his heir, then so be it. They had a young, strong king. They would have Rudolf, a man with enough royal blood to stand in the heir's place until then. Now, if their neighbours would just stop attacking them for no good reason, Reidar might be able to get his people a little peace. For he knew he should have no peace from his mother until he was wed. And maybe not even then.

<h1 style="text-align:center">Seven</h1>

In the flurry of activity around the new Lord Shoemaker, Sativa slipped away before her welling tears fell. The crown princess could not cry before the court.

She barely made it to the corridor before tears blurred her vision, but there was no one to see her distress as she fled to her chamber. A chamber she had once shared with her sisters, but was now cold and empty.

No one had lit a fire in here, and horror enveloped Sativa as she realised why. She was not meant to return here tonight – she was supposed to spend the night in her new husband's chamber. Crushed under the body of some shoemaker, as they consummated a marriage she did not want. Had not agreed to. Would never agree to, while she was betrothed to Prince Reidar of Viken.

Her fingers flew to the ring she wore on a thong about her throat, a solid reminder of the boy she had not seen since their betrothal. The prince would be a man grown now, strong enough to challenge the shoemaker for his rightful bride.

The thought of Reidar made her smile through her tears. He would ride up on his charger, wearing armour like the knights who'd come to fight the dragon. Only he would come to fight for her honour, and her love. He would make short work of the shoemaker, before lifting Sativa herself in his arms and carrying her off to his kingdom.

Her heart swelled at the thought. Yes, yes! Reidar would save her.

Sativa darted to the table and seized a quill, then searched for a clean piece of parchment. She would write him a letter, telling him about the dragon and the shoemaker and Reidar would come…

Too late.

Because her father would have her marry the shoemaker tonight. Tonight, the lowborn boy would take her maidenhead and make her miserable. Would Reidar even want someone so tainted when he arrived weeks later? What if she was carrying the shoemaker's child?

Sativa shuddered. She would not give her body to a man who did not deserve it. Who did not love her. Better to be devoured by a dragon, like her sisters had been, than that.

As long as she stayed in the castle, she would not escape this marriage. Her father would force her to it, for he could not go back on his word.

But Sativa refused to go back on her word. She'd promised to wed Reidar, and she would. She'd leave the castle tonight, and by the time her father realised she was missing, she would be far from his walls. There was no time for farewells, and who would listen, anyway? Her sisters were dead, and her father had given her away like some bauble. No, there was nothing for her here.

Down went the quill. Instead, she collected what coins she could find. Her sisters had no need for money now, and she had no idea what the price would be for passage to Reidar's kingdom, she told herself as she pawed through the chests containing her sisters' belongings. For if he could not come to her, she would go to him. With him, she would be safe.

She bundled together some spare clothes, then donned a cloak in the hope that it would hide her. Sativa paused for a moment to say a silent farewell to her sisters' spirits and the home she had known for all her life, before she turned her back on it forever.

<h1 style="text-align:center">Eight</h1>

Sativa had managed to saddle her mare, Salt, and fasten the saddlebags to the animal, when she heard approaching footsteps. Swearing silently, she slid into the stall with Salt, praying that the intruder would go away. She held her breath as she peered through the gaps in the stall wall.

Whoever it was did not respond to prayers, for they came into the stable. One of the squires, she thought at first, until the squire came into view.

Sativa almost swore again as she recognised the flaming hair of the woman the shoemaker had been staring at all night. The one who'd been so indispensable at slaying all those monsters. She would not let her lord's bride escape.

"Who's there?" the woman demanded, sliding her dagger from its sheath. "Show yourself!"

Sativa sidled deeper into the stall, hoping the woman wouldn't see her. She refused to be dragged back to the hall, to be a prize for the shoemaker. The straw shifted under her boots and Sativa nearly fell on her behind, but caught herself in time. Salt lifted her head from her dinner and snorted at Sativa, blowing fragments of straw everywhere.

Sativa gasped in horror, the worst thing she could possibly do.

The tickle started in her nose, building until it was unbearable, as if an angry bee had lodged up there and wanted out. Sativa couldn't stop it. She couldn't.

She sneezed.

Damned pea straw.

The door to the stall flew open, and the flame-haired woman stood in the breach, blocking Sativa's escape.

Sativa kept her head down, hoping the woman wouldn't recognise her, doing her best to keep the horse between them.

"Princess?"

Too late. The shoemaker's woman was an observant one.

"Why are you not at the feast, celebrating with everyone else?" she asked.

Because there was nothing to celebrate. Not any more. And this woman would not stop her. Sativa took a deep breath, fighting back another sneeze, and told the woman so.

Her dark eyes widened in surprise. And disbelief. For who could blame her? A princess's life must seem like paradise to a commoner.

Sativa continued, "I am not a prize to be won. I will not be handed to that shoemaker in marriage like some pretty bauble." She wanted to say that she would challenge anyone who tried to stop her, but Sativa was no fighter. This woman walked like a cat on the hunt — the way swordsmen stalked each other in the practice yard. So Sativa closed her mouth and glared instead.

The woman didn't seem to notice. "George is no mere shoemaker," she said slowly. Then she gave the tiniest smile. "True, he was once a master shoemaker. But he is also a hero, a slayer of monsters and giants. He has saved maidens and whole towns from monsters. And he slayed a dragon at the very gates to your city. Your father has seen fit to make him a lord and give him lands to match. Any girl would be lucky to be allowed to marry such a man." Her voice swelled with pride as her smile beamed across the stable.

This woman wanted to be the lucky girl, Sativa realised. She wanted to marry the shoemaker, and from the way her eyes flashed, she considered Sativa her rival.

Could they come to some sort of arrangement? If the woman let Sativa go free, then she would be free to marry the man she wanted.

"I will not be a prize," Sativa said. When the woman didn't seem to understand what she meant, Sativa continued, "He does not love me. Though I sat beside him, he scarcely even looked at me. He had eyes for only one person in the feasting hall. You. The one he calls his squire, but you are more than that, aren't you? You are his lover."

Any normal woman would blush at such bluntness – Sativa even felt her own cheeks grow hot – but this woman looked like she wanted to laugh.

Instead, she glanced around, before lowering her voice to say, "I am not his lover. I am his partner, in that we slayed the dragon together. We have slayed many beasts together, but I think his hero days are done."

"Lover or not, his heart belongs to you," Sativa stressed. Would the woman force Sativa to lower herself to her level and make a bargain with a commoner? Sativa tried again. "You shall not stop me. I ride to the coast, and my betrothed. A man who loves me, or at least he did once."

For who could know what Reidar thought of her now? She had not seen him since their betrothal.

A smile flickered across the woman's face so fast Sativa thought she had imagined it. Then her expression turned serious as she looked the princess up and down with a practiced eye.

"Take only what you need with you," the woman said. "Food, water, weapons, and clothes that are suited for rough travel. Nothing that will mark you for what you are, because there are men on the roads who will take advantage of a lady. They will see you as even more of a prize."

Sativa drew in a deep breath, wanting to shout at the woman that she was no one's prize.

The woman finished, "You would be safer

in your father's castle."

Sativa saw red. Safer married to a shoemaker? Forced to share his bed? "What would you know of it? A girl pretending to be a squire knows nothing of the cage that is a royal court."

This time, the woman laughed. A ladylike laugh, Sativa realised uneasily, just like her mother had taught her. And then she dropped the tiniest curtsey, as though she wore a gown and not a man's garb. The kind of curtsey a princess might offer her equal.

After a moment, the woman wiped her eyes. "Forgive me, Your Royal Highness, but I was raised in a royal court, a princess in all but name, alongside Queen Margareta's own children. And I could take my place at her side again tomorrow, if I wished. But I will not leave these walls without my armour, my weapons, and enough money and provisions for the journey, because I know there are monsters out there." She drew a dagger from its ankle sheath and held it out to Sativa. "Take it, Princess, for I promise you will have need of it."

Sativa swept aside her cape, revealing two sheathed daggers strapped to her girdle. "I am not a fool." Even if she now felt like one. How had she not noticed the woman's cultivated speech? And why would a woman so highborn want to marry a shoemaker?

The woman fumbled through her bag and pulled out a cloth bundle that she thrust at Sativa. "Then at least take these. Court dresses will be no use to you on your journey."

Sativa glanced down. She still wore her feast dress – how could she have been so stupid? She should have changed into something less showy. She should have bribed some other girl to wear her gown, to pretend to be her at the feast.

Here before her was another girl. But would she wear the gown?

Sativa took the clothing. "I thank you. But I must repay you, and I will need all the coin I have for my journey, as you say. Wait."

She worried that she was making a terrible mistake as she stripped off her silk dress and put on the other girl's clothes. They were made of cloth as fine as anything else Sativa wore, and hardly scratched at all. A blessing. But to dress as a man…Sativa had to force herself to leave the stall, stepping out into the strange woman's scrutiny.

"They are finer than they look," Sativa managed to say. She bundled up her gown and thrust it at the woman. "Here, consider this a gift."

"I have no need for silk," the woman replied, dismissing it as nothing more than an ill-fitting gown. She was a fine lady indeed in her homeland. "Oh, no. I cannot wear this."

Sativa was growing desperate. Every moment she delayed, she came closer to being caught. "Every priest in the city is so drunk they cannot tell the difference between one woman and another. Yet in an hour, my father will command one of them to conduct a wedding, marrying me to the shoemaker. If you wear this, they will think you are me. Marry the man, if that is your wish. By morning, it will be too late for anyone to do anything. I will be gone and you will be his wife." Sativa's eyes implored her. "Please."

"My lady? Are you here, or am I too late?" a male voice called.

The shoemaker.

Sativa's breath caught in her throat. He was looking for her. "He cannot catch me here. He will stop me!"

To her credit, the woman did not hesitate. She took the gown from Sativa's unresisting fingers, tucked it under her arm and winked at the princess. Then she marched out of the stables.

"Lord George," Sativa heard the woman say.

"Thank God," George said. "I thought you'd left. Melitta, I swear I didn't know about the princess. I must speak to the king, tell him I cannot…"

Sativa waited until their voices had died

away before she turned to fasten her saddlebags and check that she'd saddled her horse correctly. She rarely had to do it without the help of a groom, but needs must. Finally, she summoned the courage to leave the stables, leading Salt.

There was no one in sight as she swung onto the mare's back, but movement caught her eye and she stilled.

A door swung open, and a lady stepped out. A lady in a shimmery silk gown, with embroidery that drank the light of the torches in the courtyard, glowing gold as if by magic. It was Sativa's gown, but it was Melitta's now.

A man bowed low before her. The shoemaker. "My lady," he said throatily.

Sativa's breath caught in her throat. No man had ever spoken to her with such emotion in his voice. If Reidar loved her half that much, she would be a fool to delay. She wished the shoemaker and his lady well, but she could not stay to see more.

Sativa spurred her horse into a trot, not

daring to look back as she departed into the welcome darkness.

Nine

"Even if your girl hasn't been eaten by the dragon, the beast will take her from you all the same," Regina announced as she swept into Reidar's solar.

Reidar set down the report he'd been trying to read. "Explain yourself, Mother," he said, trying not to grit his teeth. He failed, naturally.

"Word has reached the city that he has increased the reward. Whoever slays the pesky dragon shall have half the kingdom and be named the highest lord in the land." Regina spread her hands wide. "Well, we all know what that means."

Reidar sighed. "No, I do not. Speak plainly."

Regina gave an exaggerated sigh, as if to demonstrate she'd been doing it for far longer than her son, and was far more skilled, too. "Half the kingdom is the usual dowry that comes with a princess's hand in marriage. If your girl lives, she's the other part of the prize."

"King Boreslas would not do something so dishonourable as to break the betrothal without offering me some sort of recompense. He would not offer my bride as a prize without consulting me." Reidar picked up his scroll and pretended to concentrate on it.

"Perhaps the letter has gotten lost. There are plenty of pirates on the sea between here and Kasmirus, my son. Six ships have not arrived in port, and there was no storm to delay them." Regina nodded in satisfaction, as though she was the siren who had lured these ships to their doom.

Reidar almost laughed at the image of his mother, sitting on a rock without her clothes, singing for ships full of common sailors.

"When our neighbours stop raiding our borders, and you stop wasting my time with tavern gossip, perhaps I shall have time to wipe out the pirates," Reidar snapped. "Perhaps you should take a ship out and fight the pirates yourself. I'm sure they would find you a formidable enemy." He didn't hide his fierce grin.

"You're as insolent as your father was," Regina snapped back.

Now Reidar truly did laugh. "It must be something that comes with kingship, for you've never told me that before. Now, leave me alone, Mother."

Regina marched out the door.

Insolent. Well, she'd called him worse. Only now did he let the rest of her words sink in, and Reidar began to worry.

Desperate times called for things no man would normally do. Breaking a betrothal was a small thing, when your whole kingdom was beset by a dragon as dangerous as Boreslas' one was reputed to be. A king who would offer half his kingdom to the slayer of such a fearsome beast was a desperate man indeed. Perhaps Reidar should offer Boreslas some of his own best warriors to assist him. He had lost many men fighting the dragon, and it was the mark of a good ally to help when needed. Perhaps when the winter snows set in, and his marauding neighbours decided to stay home, he would venture across the water with a band of warriors. He could defeat the dragon and claim his bride, who would look on him as her hero, for he would have saved her father's kingdom.

He laughed softly at himself. Why, he'd grown quite sentimental for a moment there. Almost as though he was in love with Princess Sativa, the woman he hadn't seen since she was a child. Was she comely, now, with the kind of curves a man wanted? Would she still have her childish fire, refined to something more queenly? Would she have turned from rebellious daughter to obedient wife? Somehow, Reidar doubted it. Oh, she might be beautiful enough to put the sun and moon to shame, and she was born to be a queen, but if she was to rule here she would need every spark of stubbornness she'd possessed as a child, stoked up to a roaring blaze. The women of Viken were as fierce as their men, and Sativa would lead by example as their queen.

Or he would have to give in to his mother's increasingly strident demands that he marry a Viken girl. And in choosing one, he would offend the families of all the girls he'd overlooked.

Not for the first time, he prayed that his envoy would bring his bride safely to him soon. Unharmed, uneaten, unmarried.

Then he returned to the report in his hands, because as long as a monarch lives, his job never ends.

Ten

Sativa watched the sailors loading up the ship, wincing as the captain bawled orders, before she summoned the courage to address the man.

"I seek passage to the sea, and onward to Viken," she announced.

The captain grunted, then turned to face her.

Sativa was tempted to turn away from his scrutiny, but what was this man to cow her? She stood firm and jingled her purse. "I can pay."

"We already have a passenger," he said. "What's your name, girl?"

Girl. Sativa longed to tell him who she was, but she wouldn't get far if she did. She glanced down at her borrowed clothes, then jerked her chin up. "Lady Melitta. I helped Lord George slay the dragon."

The captain's eyes widened. "If you don't mind sharing, mayhap we do have space. I'm Captain Ziemowit. You can call me Ziemo, my lady." He executed a stiff bow.

Praying that she wouldn't be called to slay anything, Sativa followed him aboard. At the back of the boat was a wooden cabin, not much larger than Salt's stall. Sativa had to duck her head to go inside.

"What is it, Captain?" a fretful female voice asked. "Will no one let me mourn in peace?"

"We have another passenger. An important lady. She avenged your husband, she did, and all those others the dragon took." Captain Ziemo cast Sativa an adoring look. "I watched the battle from this very deck. While the menfolk fell, she stood firm and faced that dragon to its death."

So Sativa's suspicions were true. The squire had been the true hero. Sativa wished she'd thanked the woman, but it was too late now.

"Very well," the woman said, rolling over in her bunk to squint at Sativa. "I have no maid, so the other bunk is free. It is no less comfortable than mine, for I have tried them both. I am Lady Nekane, or I was, before the dragon killed my husband, Sir Hurik. If he had but waited a day…" She sighed heavily. "Now I must go to my sister, for I have no one and nothing else. He spent all our funds on new armour to protect him against the dragon, but it was not enough."

Sativa inclined her head to the widow. "I am sorry for your loss. No doubt, your husband waits for you in heaven now, at peace with all the other lost heroes."

"Yes, yes!" Lady Nekane said, then dissolved into tears.

The captain shook his head and backed out of the cramped cabin. Sativa followed him.

She pulled out her purse. "How much do I owe you?"

Captain Ziemo waved away her coins. "Nothing, my lady. My ship is at your disposal. The least I can do for the dragonslayer. The honour of meeting you is enough. We have a full cargo, and she has paid for the cabin. If you do not mind the weeping. If you do, I could put her ashore and tell her to find passage on another ship."

Abandon a widow in such grief? Never. Sativa shook her head. "Fate has been cruel enough to her. Let her stay."

The captain bowed. "As you wish, my lady. I shall have your things brought aboard. Where are they?"

Sativa hefted the small sack she'd removed from her saddlebags. "This is all I have. I travel light, for I am going home." She prayed this would not be a lie. Reidar's castle would be her home. It had to be.

Eleven

By morning, Nekane's constant crying had nearly driven Sativa mad. Sativa wanted to scream at the woman that she'd lost all four of her sisters and almost been married off to a stranger because of the dragon. At least her late husband had chosen to fight the beast. But Sativa understood grief better than most, after losing so much more. Grief paid no heed to reason or sense, especially when it was so fresh. Why, Nekane had not been a widow for more than two days.

So Sativa spent most of her time on deck, staying out of the way of the crew as they occasionally adjusted the sails. There was less of this than she expected, for the current carried them seaward.

When the endless fields gave way to forest, Sativa wanted to cheer, because she wasn't sneezing any more. But it grew hot and still between the trees, with no breeze reaching the river, so the sailors rolled the sail up and tied it the beam at the top of the mast, and there they stayed.

Sativa approached the captain. "What are they doing?" she asked.

He shaded his eyes from the sun and looked up. "Catching the breeze, perhaps, or admiring the view. 'Tis cooler up there than on deck. I'd be up there myself, but someone must steer the ship."

There was a cool place on the ship? Sativa tugged her sweat-soaked tunic away from her skin for what felt like the dozenth time. She longed to be in the tower room she'd shared with her sisters, wearing little more than linen shifts in the heat. But there would be no such days again. Her sisters were dead, and she would never go back.

"They'll make space for you if you wish to join them, my lady," Captain Ziemo said, evidently mistaking the look of longing on her face. He cupped his hands to his mouth and shouted, "Move aside there. The lady is coming up!"

Sativa opened her mouth to protest. Surely it was too high and too dangerous. Her mother would have screamed aloud at the very thought. And her father…

No longer cared. He'd handed her over to the shoemaker.

Lady Melitta would do it, a sly thought whispered through her mind. It was true. Lady Melitta would be up the mast in no time. Why, the woman had defeated a dragon and who knew what else. The captain would think less of her if she did not.

Sativa swallowed and made her way to the

mast. It was just a dead tree, she told herself. She'd climbed plenty of trees as a child, until her sisters had tried to copy her and Viola had broken her arm in a bad fall. Then her mother had banned them all from such things. Since her mother died, Sativa had never felt the need to disobey her. Until now.

Someone had cut notches into the mast, which made it a much easier climb. Sativa had to stretch for some of them, for they'd evidently been cut with a man's longer limbs in mind, but she managed until she grasped the sail. That's when she made the mistake of looking down.

Sativa swore.

The men around her laughed. "I didn't know ladies knew words like that," one of them said.

Sativa felt her face grow hot. If she were still alive, her mother would be ashamed of her.

"Don't look down, lady," a boy who could not be more than ten years old told her. "Hook your elbows over the yard and hang onto the shroud." He demonstrated, and so did the others.

They all looked like men being crucified, Sativa thought uneasily, as she dug her fingers into the folded sail. But crucifixion took days to kill a man, and they wouldn't be up here that long, she told herself.

And there was a breeze up there, she was pleased to find, as it caressed her face. She was level with the treetops, and she could see the forest stretching for miles on either side of her.

"Ooh, an eagle! Look!" The man pointed.

Sativa's eyes followed his finger. Sure enough, the enormous bird wheeled above the forest, too intent on its prey below to pay any attention to a ship sailing along the river. Or perhaps the regal bird simply did not care.

She envied the animal its graceful calm as it glided across the sky. She would never be so free. And yet, for the moment, she soared above the river, thanks to the ship that carried her to her destiny.

Twelve

Sativa spent most of her time atop the mast, where one of the men had nailed a little platform for her feet to rest on. She only descended when she had to – for mealtimes, and at night, when she ventured into the cabin she shared with Nekane so that she might sleep.

Nekane never noticed if she was there or not, and Sativa was hardly the person to comfort a grieving widow. If her plans came to pass, she would soon be happily married to a man she had no intention of losing to a dragon. If there were any such beasts left in the world. Sativa certainly hoped not.

Sativa was aloft when she heard the cry, "Captain! There's a ship in trouble ahead!"

The lookout on her left pointed.

Ahead of them, the river curved around a bend, and it appeared that a ship had taken that bend so fast, it had tipped over. Perhaps that was to be expected in such a strange boat, which looked very little like the broad-beamed river boat Sativa travelled on. The craft lay on its side, looking for all the world like a bowl a giant had sat on, squashing the usually flat base until it folded into a ridge at the bottom, and forcing the sides up like a sort of funnel. If it weren't for the pointy bits at either end, and the mast in the middle, Sativa would be hard pressed to recognise it as a boat at all.

It had ropes tied to it in several places, which stretched across the water and the shore, where dozens of people were trying to right the stricken vessel.

"We'll anchor here for the night," Captain Ziemo shouted, pointing. "Surely that little fishing village has a tavern, eh?"

The men cheered, and Sativa had never seen them work so fast. Even Sam, the cabin boy, seemed excited to be going ashore.

Sativa considered going with them. After all, when would she ever have another opportunity to visit a fishing village, or a tavern?

Almost as though the captain had read her mind, he turned to her. "Lady Melitta," he said gravely, "Would you be kind enough to watch over my vessel while we're gone? We will be under way in the morning, I promise you, as soon as the way is clear once more." He gestured at the stricken ship.

Sativa didn't know what to say. She wasn't sure if Melitta was familiar with ships, but after listening to the shoemaker's stories of her, there was little the woman could not do. Finally, she said, "I…I am not a particularly experienced mariner, Captain Ziemo. But if the ship should sink while you are gone, I will be certain to swim to shore, so that I might point to where your vessel lies."

Ziemo's eyes widened in surprise, before he let out a roar of laughter. "A good jest indeed, my lady. But my *Wydra* is sound as a drum. The only water in her bilges is the sweat of the men who work aboard her, I promise you."

"Men you promised some shore leave, Captain!" one of the men shouted as they lowered the boats over the side. Within moments, they'd climbed down the side of the ship and into the two boats, stranding Sativa on the ship with Nekane.

Rather than sit in the cabin with the endlessly weeping widow, Sativa climbed to her perch atop the mast and watched the men trying to save their ship.

It had run aground in the shallows, she saw now, and while the ship might look strange to her eyes, it did not appear to be damaged. She expected splintered planks or some part of it to be stove in, but instead it just lay there, like a toy boat some giant child had discarded, waiting for the boy to return for it so that he might make more mischief in the duck pond.

After plenty of pulling and shouting that achieved nothing, the men stretched out on the shore, opened a barrel of something, and started to drink. Someone lit a fire, and it soon had a stewpot suspended above it. Though she could not smell it, Sativa imaged the stew would smell delicious around about now.

She sighed. Their ship's cook had gone ashore with everyone else, so she would have to see to her own dinner for once. Descending to the deck, she helped herself to the ship's provisions. As she ate, she prayed that Reidar kept a good cook. More often than not, the meals aboard the ship were so bad, they had almost made her wish she was home in her father's hall. Almost, but not quite. So she choked down enough food to keep hunger at bay, and waited for the day when her ordeal would be over.

When the sun started to sink, one of the

men on the other side of the river gave a shout. The others came to stand with him, staring at the grounded ship. Unable to hear what they were saying or see what captivated their attention, Sativa ascended the mast once more.

Waves lapped at the ship now, lifting it as all the assembled men had not managed to. Even as Sativa watched, it started to right itself. It was the tide coming in, she realised. She'd heard of such things, but never seen them until now.

She watched in fascination as the men worked with the tide to refloat their ship. Even she felt pride swell in her heart as the masts rose so high in the sky they were silhouetted against the rising moon. The ship was saved!

She felt the thump of booted feet on the deck below. The crew had returned early, perhaps to take advantage of the turning of the tide and the cleared channel. Best to stay aloft and out of their way as they readied the ship to sail, she decided. So Sativa watched the stars come out instead, some as faint as a whisper and others as bright as a trumpet blast in the sky. Movement caught her eye, and she watched in wonderment as a star shot across the sky like an arrow, then vanished.

What had her nurse said about such things? Were they a good omen, or bad? Sativa racked her brain until she found the answer. They were not omens at all, but wishes. The one who sees such a star must make a wish.

Quickly, she squeezed her eyes shut and wished with every spark in her soul that she would reach Reidar safely and soon.

"Please, oh please, leave me be!" a female voice begged.

Sativa glanced down at the deck. "Quiet, you," a rough male voice said, followed by the smack of skin against flesh.

Nekane cried out.

Sativa stiffened. What man would dare strike a lady? Not Captain Ziemo, certainly, or one of his crew. They were honourable men, or so she'd thought. She should do something.

But what? She was no match for most of them, except maybe young Sam, the cabin boy. She might pretend to be Melitta, but Sativa was no warrior. She'd been taught to command men with her voice alone, for what more did a queen need?

She wet her lips, wondering what to say. What if the man was too drunk to listen, and turned on her instead?

It did not matter. No man should strike a lady.

"Leave her alone," Sativa said, or tried to. Her firm tone came out as more of a squeak.

"Who's there?" the man growled, lifting a lantern high. His other hand tightened around Nekane's arm, until the woman whimpered. "Show yourself, boy!"

Boy? Sativa seethed.

"What's the matter, Karl?" another voice asked.

Nekane's captor jerked his chin upward. "There's a boy atop the mast, Captain."

"Come down, boy, or we'll shoot you

down!" the second voice boomed. It did not belong to Captain Ziemo.

Better to be obedient than dead, Sativa told herself as she descended. Her feet hadn't even touched the deck when a rough hand grabbed her arm and almost knocked her off her feet.

"What's your name, boy?" the hand's owner asked, bringing his hairy face so close to Sativa's that she could smell his breath. Not that she wanted to.

She coughed. "Sam," she said weakly.

"Want me to kill young Sam here, Captain?" Bad Breath asked. He shook Sativa until her teeth rattled.

The captain's hat cast a shadow over his face as his hulking shoulder loomed above Sativa. "Bring him along. We could do with a new cabin boy. Lost the last one, didn't we?"

The men laughed. Only now did Sativa realise there were more than three of them. There were at least a dozen – more than the crew of the *Wydra* – all carrying casks and chests from the ship's hold.

"You're pirates!" she cried, hating how her voice still squeaked with fear. No wonder they thought her a boy. "Stealing from Captain Ziemo – he won't stand for it!"

More laughter. "Your captain's drunk under a table, along with the rest of his crew. Strong brew they sell in the taverns hereabouts. Too strong for you. So what'll it be, boy? You can come with us or I'll cut your throat and throw you over the side. Plenty more boys who'd kill to be cabin boy on a pirate ship. More wealth than you'll ever see on a tub like this."

Pirates. So much for her wish for safety. Sativa swallowed. "I always wanted to be a pirate cabin boy," she whispered.

"Good choice. Now get them both to the boat, and see that they stay there." Someone gave Sativa a push, toward the side of the ship.

Peering over the gunwale, Sativa could just make out the boats lying in the *Wydra*'s shadow. Below her, a bulky shape swung away from the ship and landed in the boat. The man leaned forward and dropped a bundle on the bottom of the boat. The bundle yelped.

Nekane.

Sativa couldn't leave her alone with these pirates. Summoning what courage she had left, she swung her leg over the side and felt around for the rope ladder she knew had hung there in daylight. She'd never climbed down anything so frightening in her life. Slapping against the hull of the ship, splashed by waves, until hands grabbed her around the middle and hauled her aboard a boat. But not the boat that held Nekane – another one, full of chests that left her nowhere to sit but on top of one.

Sativa drew a deep, shaky breath. This would not end well.

Thirteen

Reidar paced the tower, unable to stay still. He could see several ships from the windows, but he knew none of them could be hers. Not yet. His envoy would have just arrived in Kasmirus, if he hadn't met with any delays. He probably hadn't even seen King Boreslas yet. So it was too much to hope that she might be aboard one of the vessels in view.

And yet…

Reidar sighed. He'd dreamed of her last night. She'd had golden hair as a girl, the same colour as the straw that made her sneeze, so the beauty in his dreams had been blonde, too. She'd stood in the crow's nest atop the mast, her hair streaming behind her like a pennant in the breeze. As eager to glimpse him as he was to see her. Then she'd slid down that mast as lithely as any sailor, her curves hugging the wood like he wished they'd mould to him. And she'd run across the dock, her boots hammering on the timber as she flew toward him, her arms outspread like wings…

And then he'd woken up to realise that the hammering was not in his head, but outside, as some fisherman felt the need to mend his boat below Reidar's window.

By then, his dream bride was gone, for dreams were no more than moonbeams, and he was alone in his bed, longing for a lady he barely knew with no idea of what she even looked like now.

What would his men say, if they knew? They'd think him a fool, to be so besotted with a woman. A woman he hadn't seen in years.

Did she think of him at all, or had she forgotten him entirely? He wanted to believe she'd kept her promise, and the ring he'd given her, but his gift was likely lost among dozens of others from her many suitors, men who might be wooing her even now, while he was far away. Oh, they might be betrothed, but a woman's heart was far stronger than any childhood promise. Especially one she'd likely forgotten. If only he could stand before her and remind her.

Curse this war! Why couldn't his neighbours be content with their borders, and let him sit on his throne in peace for just a little while? A few summer raids were one thing, little more than fun and friendly rivalry between his men and theirs. But this…trying to claim his throne as their own, and his lands as well? These northerners had no idea who they were dealing with. They must think him some weak boy, easily set aside. If he was to join the war against him, they would soon learn he was as much a warrior as his father.

Reidar clapped his hands and laughed aloud. Were there anyone in earshot, they would think him mad, but he didn't care. He knew the cure for worrying about a woman. He would go to war, as his ancestors had. In the heat of battle, he'd have no cravings for a woman's warmth. Just a sword and a shield, waiting to sing a song of victory over his fallen foes. With an army at his back, of course. He might be a fool when it came to women, but not when it came to war.

Fourteen

The boat carrying Nekane arrived at the ship first – the very same vessel that had lain on its side for most of the day, if Sativa was not mistaken. It bobbed about in the waves as though it had taken no damage from its stranding, and now she was about to climb aboard it, Sativa certainly hoped it was as sound as Captain Ziemo's *Wydra*.

She glanced back, to see the *Wydra* still floating in its anchorage, though much higher in the water, thanks to the things the pirates had taken from her.

She'd heard that pirates sank ships, and killed all those aboard, after taking anything of value, of course. If they hadn't scuttled the *Wydra* and she and Nekane were still alive, perhaps these were not the sort of pirates she'd heard horrible tales about. Men of honour, maybe, who would take her to Reidar when she told them who she was.

"Take her to the captain's cabin," a voice said, carrying across the waves.

"No, no, please no…" Nekane pleaded as she was hoisted up onto the ship.

They were taking her to the best accommodations aboard, Sativa told herself. She would expect the same, once they knew she was a princess. Or even if she told them she was Lady Melitta.

"Up you go, boy," a man said, shoving her toward the ship.

Sativa stared up. This rope ladder stretched a lot higher than the one on the *Wydra*, but she would have to climb it, or be carried up like a sack of grain, as Nekane had. Judging by Nekane's protests, it wasn't a comfortable ride.

With one burly man above her on the ladder and another behind, at least she couldn't fall, Sativa told herself. Their weight kept the ladder from moving too much, too.

By the time Sativa hauled herself over the side of the ship and onto the deck, her arms were screaming a protest at having to work so hard. But none of the men complained, so she stayed silent.

Someone clapped her on the back so hard she nearly fell over.

Laughter erupted around her. "Boy's asleep on his feet. Wake up, boy. You'll get no rest until we get this cargo stowed."

Cargo? Oh, the things they'd stolen from the *Wydra*. Chests and casks she could not hope to lift. What had possessed her to tell them she'd be their cabin boy? Sativa should tell them the truth now.

"Captain's aboard!" The shout had all men bowing their heads as the hulking shadow stepped over the gunwale and onto the deck.

"Where's the boy?" the shadow growled.

Sativa was shoved forward again. "Here, Captain Zydrunas," someone behind her said.

A lantern was thrust toward her face, so close she feared it might burn her. Sativa cringed away.

"You ever sailed before, boy?" Captain Zydrunas demanded.

"N-no," Sativa stammered. "This was my first time."

"Can you lift a cask?"

Sativa wanted to say no, but some darkness in his tone gave her pause. Instead, she knelt and tried to lift the nearest barrel. She managed to tip it a little toward her, before she overbalanced and went down with the cask on top of her.

The laughter was louder this time as the crew took their time rescuing her from the heavy barrel.

"Take him below decks, and show him where he can sleep. Maybe he'll be more useful in the morning," Captain Zydrunas said.

Someone hustled Sativa down the steps below the deck, into a room that stretched from one side of the ship to the other. She had to duck her head to enter, and couldn't straighten once she was in, for the ceiling was too low. She bumped into something cold and hard, as high as her waist. Moonlight streamed through a gap in the wall, revealing the object to be a cannon, its mouth pointed through the hole. There was a whole row of cannons on each side, muzzles extended outward like gargoyles, or guard dogs ready to bite. Above them hung hammocks, stretched between the posts holding up the ceiling.

"That one's free, boy," a strange voice said. It sounded older than the others, and a whole lot friendlier. An arm extended from a hammock in the corner, pointing at the opposite corner. Sure enough, there was no sea chest below that one, like there were under the others.

"Thank you," she mumbled, picking her way

carefully over the clutter of cannonballs, chests and other assorted things she never knew lurked below decks. It took her a few tries to get herself into the hammock, but when she finally managed it, she found the hanging bed surprisingly comfortable. Better than a straw pallet like the sailors on the *Wydra* slept on, too, for it didn't make her sneeze.

Sativa closed her eyes and settled herself for sleep.

"NOOOOOOOO!"

A piecing scream tore the air above her.

Sativa thrashed, floundered, and fell out of her hammock onto the floor. "What in heaven's name is that?" she cried.

But the building dread in her heart whispered an answer she didn't want to believe.

The old man in the corner piped up, "The captain's new bedwarmer, I expect. They all scream like that until he's broken them in. Sometimes, when he's done with her, he lets the crew have a woman for a while. You ever had a woman, boy?"

Nekane's screams seemed to reach inside Sativa and slice through her heart. Right above her, the captain was raping that poor widow. A lady. And when he was finished, he'd give her to the crew. So that they might do the same. Like she was some sort of whore.

Sativa shivered. Part of her wanted to try to save the woman, but she knew it was no use. She wasn't strong enough to lift a barrel, let alone fight the whole crew of a pirate ship. And if they found out she was a woman…then what? If she couldn't save Nekane, Sativa would be next.

No. If Sativa lay with another man before she married Reidar, even unwillingly, there would be no wedding. Bile rose in her throat at the thought of her own cowardice as Sativa huddled in her hammock, wishing the screaming would stop.

"A smart woman would take her own life before letting herself be taken aboard a pirate ship, eh, boy?" the old man cackled. "But most women aren't smart. Too soft to take a dagger to their breast. But their softness is the best bit."

The screaming continued long into the night, as Sativa cried silent tears, cursing her own stupidity for landing her in such a situation. Then her thoughts turned to Nekane, and what the other woman must be suffering, and Sativa got no sleep at all.

Fifteen

By morning, Sativa's horror-filled mind had only one goal: to be the best, most convincing cabin boy she could be until the ship approached shore…and then she would escape as fast as her feet could sprint. She soon learned that the old man who'd helped her the previous night was the ship's cook, and his culinary skills made the food she'd eaten on the *Wydra* seem like ambrosia.

After this journey was over, she swore, she'd never take fruit or fresh-baked bread for granted again.

The best provisions the pirates had stolen from their victims belonged to the captain's table alone. Sativa thought of the horrible price Nekane had to pay to sup at that table, and shuddered. She could subsist on hardtack, dried fish and endless pickled cabbage for a little while, if it meant not having to share the captain's cabin.

After that first night, Nekane's screams had fallen silent, and Sativa hadn't heard her make a sound since. Not a sob, a complaint…nothing. The widow hadn't come out of the cabin, either, though she was certainly still there. In the absence of screaming, Sativa could hear the regular beat of the captain rutting in the bed above her hammock every night.

Some of the other men took this as a hint to pleasure themselves in their hammocks, a mentality that made Sativa feel even sicker. That one man could take pleasure in forcing an unwilling woman was one thing…but a whole crew who got excited at the mere idea of it? It was enough to keep her shuddering in her bunk for the rest of the voyage. Yet she could not stay below decks – as cabin boy, she had work to do.

Cook made her fetch and carry things up from the hold that he wanted. At first, it was just ordinary staples for the crew's meals, but then he started sending her down for the captain's special stores. Soon, she knew where everything was kept, and she began to plan. She set aside something each day – a skin of wine here, a dried sausage there – in a small cask behind the enormous tun of pickled cabbage.

As soon as they were within sight of shore, she'd wait until nightfall, load her supplies into a boat, and head for land. The one thing she hadn't found yet was coin – she'd need money to reach Reidar and she'd left all hers aboard the *Wydra*. Would it truly be stealing if she took coin from pirates who'd in all likelihood stolen hers when they took everything else?

Or perhaps she could call it fair payment. After all, cabin boys got paid, didn't they? She had no idea how much, but if she took more than she should, the pirates could come find her in Reidar's castle, and she would gladly pay her debt. Right after she saw Zydrunas punished for what he'd done to Nekane.

Nekane. She'd need to save her, if she could, too. Somehow smuggle her out of the captain's cabin and into the boat. Once they reached shore, if Nekane was too weak to travel, she would find someone willing to care for her until she could return. That would mean more coin, but Sativa didn't care. What Zydrunas owed Nekane was far more than money. No price was too high.

Sixteen

Another mug of ale, Reidar judged, and he'd have well and truly drowned out the pain in his arm. Today he'd met his first berserker, an experience he didn't want to repeat. The madman had run at him, screaming, then buried his axe so deep in Reidar's shield he'd cleaved the buckler in two, nearly breaking Reidar's arm in the process. Reidar's answering blow had sliced deep into the berserker's shoulder, at the base of his neck. The man had fallen to his knees, gurgling, before he died a noisy death at Reidar's feet. Reidar had only been dimly aware of it at the time, of course, because he'd had another foe to face, but now the battle was over, the man was once again on his mind.

The berserker had claimed to be the bastard son of either his father or his grandfather, Reidar wasn't sure, which he'd believed meant the throne Reidar occupied rightly belonged to him, and all of Viken's people would come to his way of thinking once Reidar was dead.

Except Reidar wasn't dead and the bastard's blood now fertilised the field, which didn't care whose son he was. Nor did Reidar care, not truly, for the man's claim died with him. What remained of his raiding party melted away across the border, either to join other armies or head home. Or to die of their injuries along the way, for his men had been particularly ruthless today. Perhaps it made a difference that instead of just fighting for their country, today they were also fighting for their king.

It was a heady thought. He'd fought

alongside these men for weeks now, weeks he'd fought as fiercely as any of them, knowing that he fought for them as much as the land they stood upon, but this was the first time he'd understood what that meant.

They would die for him, just as he would fight for them. He was their king, and they were his men. He owned the hearts and souls and bodies of free, fighting men. Reidar only hoped that one day he would truly deserve the honour they did him. Until then, he would draw his sword alongside them, to defend what was theirs.

Now he understood how his father had died on a battlefield. It was the duty of a king to live and die for his people.

Reidar tipped up his cup, but it was empty. Sighing, he headed for the barrel to get some more ale.

"I must see the king!" an insistent voice shouted. A voice Reidar didn't recognise.

The man rode into their circle, reining his horse in so close to the fire that its hooves kicked up sparks. He slid from his mount's back with practiced ease, then planted his feet before the fire like a man staking a claim.

Reidar edged closer, carrying his full cup. Most of the men present were deep in their cups, but they loosened swords and daggers in their sheaths, ready to take this new man down if their king commanded it.

"Where is the king?" the man demanded. "'Twas he who summoned me."

Reidar didn't remember summoning anyone. He squinted at the man. There was something familiar about him, but Reidar could not place him.

"Reidar!" the man cried, breaking into a smile. He strode across the trampled grass, heedless of the men who eyed him as he passed, and embraced Reidar. "Cousin, it is good to see you! Where is the king?"

Bursts of laughter exploded around the fire. Though Reidar still didn't recognise him, this could only be one man.

"Rudolf? I thought you'd sailed off the

western edge of the world!"

Rudolf grinned even more widely. "One day, maybe I will. But those islands…I can see why our people love them so much. Their men fight just as fiercely, but so differently! We'll never conquer them as long as they live. And the women…my God, the women…"

"It's hardly fair to speak of women in a war camp where the only women are in our dreams," Reidar reproached him, forcing back the unbidden image of Sativa that had come to mind.

Rudolf clapped his hands together. "That's right! I'm not the only man who missed out on a marriage. I got summoned back here before I could ask for her, and yours got handed over as the price for a dragon's head."

"What?"

Rudolf waved his hand airily. "That foreign princess you were betrothed to. When I left Portnahaven, every man who could lift a sword was talking about the dragon of Kasmirus, and how the king there had offered half his kingdom and one of his daughters as a bride to the man who could bring him the beast's head. Everyone thought I was leaving to do battle with the beast! They seemed quite disappointed when I said I was going home. Though after so long there, it feels like the Southern Isles are more a home to me than here. Has it always been this cold?"

Reidar's heart clenched in his chest at the thought of some other man marrying Sativa, but he banished that foolish notion. "Boreslas would not break off a betrothal with me without telling me so first. He has other daughters, I am sure. He would not break an agreement with the king of Viken. Even now, my envoy is at his court, to bring me my bride."

"King? So the rumours are true? Not just my father, but yours died, too?" Rudolf bowed his head. "I am sorry for your loss, cousin. Your father was a good king, and a wise one, too. Why else would he send me to the ends of the earth to learn warcraft from some foreign lord?" He laughed. "I can tell you tales of tactics their men use in battle that we would never think of. I would not have believed them, had I not seen it with my own eyes."

"Battle tactics? But Mother said – " Reidar clamped his mouth shut, but it was too late. Even he knew it was a sign of weakness for a king to rely so heavily on his mother.

"Is Aunt Regina still around? She will outlive us all, that battle axe will. I remember she caught me sitting on your father's throne once. She clouted me over the ear and gave me such a tongue lashing I couldn't open my mouth in her presence for a year. She said if she ever caught me sitting there again, she'd thrash my backside until I had nothing left to sit on!" Rudolf laughed as though it was all a joke to him.

It had been no joke to Regina, Reidar knew. For after Reidar himself, Rudolf had the best blood claim to the throne. Was Rudolf a danger to him?

Rudolf had been just a boy when he left,

and now he was a man grown. A man Reidar did not know. But he needed to know him.

If Rudolf was loyal and no risk, Reidar could leave an army in his capable hands to harry the border raiders, and finally win this war. If he wanted the throne…giving him an army would be tantamount to handing him the country and Reidar's own head in the bargain.

"Tomorrow, we ride west, to where there are reports of a foreign force waiting to ambush us. In three days' time, we shall go into battle. Will you join us, cousin?" Reidar asked.

"The Southern Isles may have softened me, but beneath it beats a Viken heart still!" Rudolf declared. "I will fight at your side like we did as boys."

As boys, they had been closer than brothers. Reidar hoped that would still be the case, but it would be three days before he knew for sure.

"Ale for my cousin! We must toast his return!" Reidar said. A cup was fetched and filled, which Reidar then presented to Rudolf.

Rudolf took it, then managed to drop to one knee without spilling his ale. "Nay, a toast to my cousin, the new king of Viken. May his reign be long and filled with so many victories the bards forget to sing of anyone else!"

The other men shouted and joined Rudolf's toast, before proceeding to offer him food and a place at the fire.

Reidar hung back, observing all that passed. The only person in his thoughts was Rudolf, and whether he would prove to be his staunchest ally or his greatest enemy. Only time would tell.

<h1 style="text-align:center">Seventeen</h1>

Cook shoved a covered bowl into Sativa's hands. "Here. Take the captain his dinner."

Sativa almost dropped it in surprise. "The captain?"

Cook made an exasperated sound. "Yes, Captain Zydrunas, the man who commands this ship and crew. He doesn't come and fetch his food like the rest of the men — we must take it to him. And tonight, we means you. I'm far too busy to wait on him."

"Where do I take it?" Sativa asked. The

captain was usually on deck, keeping his eye on everyone, but try as she might, Sativa could not remember ever seeing the man eat.

"His cabin, of course. Knock on the door, and if there is no answer, leave it outside the door. And be quick about it, for the captain prefers his food hot."

"Then if he does not answer, I should take it into his cabin, and leave it on the table," Sativa said thoughtfully. "For if he does not like his food cold, surely – "

"Do not enter the captain's cabin," Cook interrupted. "No matter what you hear, or what you think. Either he will open the door and take the food from you, or you leave it outside. You hear me?"

Sativa mumbled a resentful response. Even after weeks at sea, she still did not take orders gladly. Cook never seemed to care if she scowled, as long as she obeyed. The other men were not so happy about it, but the more she kept out of their way, the less they had to dislike.

So she carefully carried the bowl down the ladder, trying to ignore the rumbling of her belly as she inhaled the savoury smell of the captain's dinner. When she finally found her way ashore, she would spend the first week eating everything in sight, she was sure of it. She'd even settle for some of the stuff she'd eaten aboard the *Wydra*, for that was at least food, and not the swill Cook served to this crew.

But in the meantime, she made her way to the captain's cabin. This was where he kept Nekane. Perhaps she would answer the door and Sativa could tell her about her escape plan, so Nekane might be ready when the time came.

Cradling the bowl in her arms, Sativa knocked on the door, then waited. And waited.

Surely Nekane would come to the door. Where else could she be? Unless the captain had her pinned beneath him…Sativa swallowed. Last night she'd barely slept as the rhythmic pounding from the captain in this cabin above her hadn't stopped from dusk until dawn. Surely he couldn't be at it again now. Sativa might be a virgin, but even she knew men didn't last that long in bed. A man who could manage lovemaking for more than a few minutes was a miracle by most standards, and Captain Zydrunas did not seem the type to be blessed by angels. Sold his soul to the devil, more like.

She knocked again, louder this time. Perhaps the captain had not heard her over the noises he was making.

But she received no response this time, either.

Perhaps if she brought the man his dinner, he might leave Nekane alone for a little while, Sativa told herself. She could say she'd heard him tell her to enter.

She pushed against the door, but it didn't budge. She set her shoulder against it, and shoved harder. Still nothing. It wasn't until she looked down that she saw the bolt, fastening the door shut from the outside. Nekane couldn't answer the door because she couldn't get out, Sativa realised. No wonder she hadn't seen the other woman since they'd boarded the ship. She was a prisoner in the captain's cabin.

Sativa reached down to pull the bolt open.

"What in the devil's name are you doing, boy?" a voice roared.

Sativa jumped, barely managing to keep her grip on the bowl. "Bringing you your dinner, sir," she said, shrinking against the wall to put more space between her and the captain. In these close confines, he seemed bigger than ever.

He snatched the bowl out of her hands. "I'll take that. And you are never to enter my cabin, you understand? Never. It's forbidden."

"But what about the lady?" Sativa said before she could stop herself.

The captain's face loomed so close she could see the individual strands of his blue-black beard. "What about the lady, boy?" He spat the last word as though it was some sort of epithet.

Sativa swallowed. She had to say something. "Maybe she'd like a bit of company. It must be lonely in there by herself all day," she managed to say.

Captain Zydrunas snorted. "Never you mind about the lady, boy. She has all the company she'll ever need from me."

He unbolted the door, opened it just wide enough to let him through, and vanished into the cabin, slamming the door shut behind him.

Sativa craned her neck, straining to see, but there was nothing but darkness before the door closed the view off for good. But it also meant she was out of the captain's sight. She clenched her fists, swearing she would find a way off this ship. The captain could not always be near his cabin. One day, she'd find a way to sneak in and speak to Nekane. One day, they'd both be free.

Eighteen

Steel rang against steel as Reidar blocked another blow with his sword. And another, and another. Loath though he was to admit it, the slight man before him was too fast for him. His blows lacked Reidar's strength, or perhaps he was just holding back, hoping to tire Reidar enough to win. Reidar could not let that happen.

But not even a king is infallible, he realised as something stung his side. Reidar knew better than to look down to investigate the wound, for if it did not kill him, then the next blow would, if he did not block it. With a roared oath, he renewed his attack, praying his foe would fall before he did. The trickle of blood down his side told him time was of the essence now.

"Protect the king!" a voice bellowed.

Reidar lifted his shield to take the next blow, but the man's axe met steel instead. His eyes widened in surprise, meeting Reidar's gaze. So Reidar saw his eyes glaze over as the second sword withdrew from the man's throat, turning a live enemy into a dead one.

"Thank you," Reidar said shakily.

Rudolf lifted his bloody sword in salute. "Any time, my king." He turned away to fight another foe.

Hours or maybe minutes later, Reidar could not be sure, he called the end of the battle. There were few left alive from the raiding party, and his own men had wounds that needed tending.

The slice to his side had done little more

than scrape the skin, Reidar was happy to discover, so once his wound was washed and bandaged, he had time to walk around their camp and speak to his men. Rudolf's steel helm had been so dented in the battle it took two men to pull it off his head, only to find his face covered in blood from a broken nose.

While one of the men cleaned up Rudolf's face, amid a lot of swearing from the patient, Reidar approached him. He dismissed the healer and tended Rudolf himself so that he might speak with the man privately.

"Why did you do that? Call the men to me during the battle?" Reidar asked.

Rudolf shrugged, then swore as the movement pained him. "Because it's a man's duty to protect his king. We're yours to command. There's no doubt in anyone's mind that you can fight as well as any man here, and none of us question your right to rule. But if you fall in battle, I'll have to sit on your seat, and Aunt Regina will never forgive me."

"What, you don't want a crown, cousin?"

Reidar forced out a laugh to make the question sound more flippant than it was.

Rudolf smiled, or grimaced – it was hard to tell. "Right now, I want nothing on my head at all. My ears are still ringing from the blow to my helm. I would much rather a cup of ale than a crown."

Reidar wasn't sure if this was a jest or not. It certainly wasn't an answer. Nevertheless, he called for ale for his cousin.

Rudolf seized Reidar's arm and pulled him close so that no one might hear his words. "If you die without an heir, your crown falls to me anyway. We both know this. Go back to your castle, get yourself a bride, and put a boy in her belly. Several, if you can. Let me lead the army in your stead."

Reidar met Rudolf's blackened and bloodshot eyes. There was truth in them, he was sure of it. But something hidden, too. "To what end, cousin? You have a plan, I am sure of it."

"All men plan, but not all plans bear fruit.

Rest assured, mine do not need you to die here on a battlefield like my father and yours. I want this kingdom secure as much as you do. These raiders and would-be usurpers must die!" Rudolf shook his fist in the direction the surviving raiders had retreated.

Something in Rudolf's voice urged Reidar to trust him. Maybe not completely, but for now. Reidar nodded slowly. "Very well. Will the men follow you?"

Rudolf laughed. "They did today. They're loyal men who serve their king. Why would they not?"

Reidar had to admit his cousin was right. And, if his count was correct, his envoy should have brought Sativa to Viken by now. At this very moment, she could be waiting for him in the very tower he'd built for her.

"Tonight we toast our victory, and tomorrow I shall return," Reidar said.

Rudolf winked. "Share a drink with your wife at your wedding feast, cousin, for I doubt this war will be over by then, and I wouldn't want you to delay on my account. We'll drink your health when we hear of it."

"I'll send a cask of ale from my cellars. The very best," Reidar promised. And he would. When he had Sativa safely in his arms, he would want the whole kingdom to celebrate.

Nineteen

Sativa hugged the mast as she did the one part of her job she actually liked – keeping watch. Captain Zydrunas' *Barbe* had a sort of man-sized bucket built at the top of the mast for the lookout, and Sativa would stay there all day, if she could.

It also meant she'd be the first to spot… "Land!" she cried, pointing. It looked like a just a shadow on the horizon, but it was growing larger, and she was sure…

"Check and see if the boy is right," Captain

Zydrunas ordered.

Sativa's face grew hot. Last time she'd thought she'd spotted land, it had been a bank of storm clouds. They'd steered well away from them, but the waves had been big enough for her to realise why the lookout had what the crew called a crow's nest: when the ship canted from one side to the other, it was easy for a lookout to fall into the sea and be lost, like the last cabin boy. Sativa had hung on with all her strength and stayed aboard. But today, she was sure she was right. And if she was, it would soon be time to go.

One of the younger men, barely older than Sativa herself, scaled the mast and peered in the direction she'd pointed. "The boy's right!" he shouted.

She was nameless to them, and she'd resolved they'd remain nameless to her, too. Pirate scum such as these did not deserve to be remembered. The moment she arrived on land, she would do her best to forget everything about them.

"That's the coast of Viken. You can see the Sea Tower on the cliff!"

Sativa stared across the sea, hungry for a glimpse of it. Was this the tower Reidar had promised to build for her?

But no matter how long she looked, she couldn't see it. Perhaps when they got closer.

The captain gave orders to make for Viken, and Sativa was ready to dance for joy. Perhaps she wouldn't need to steal a boat at all. Instead, she could simply walk ashore once they docked and vanish into the town. Once she was in Reidar's kingdom, surely his people would help her find him.

By the time the sun sank beneath the western waves, they were no closer to the shadowy land Sativa couldn't wait to call home, and she sank into her hammock distinctly dissatisfied.

Morning brought a renewal of hope, as she started to discern the shapes of trees and then buildings upon the shore.

"Search for somewhere we can go ashore

for water," the captain directed. "We're running low."

They weren't headed for a port after all, Sativa realised with a sinking heart. Then she would have to make a run for it when she found the opportunity. When they went ashore for water, perhaps, or at night, if no suitable stream was found.

All day they watched, sailing so close to shore Sativa could count the sheep and cows on the cliffs. Alas, the streams they did find were too hard to reach, and so they sailed on. More than once, she'd been tempted to dive from the bow and swim ashore, but she knew she would not succeed with everyone watching the shore so closely. So many men, bigger and stronger than she was, could surely swim faster, too, and they would haul her back to be punished.

She'd seen some of the punishments aboard the *Barbe* — men's backs whipped to jelly for drinking more than their share of ale, or stealing food from the captain's stores. If the captain knew how much she'd stashed away for her escape…Sativa shuddered. That was why she kept her supplies hidden, where no one could be certain who they belonged to.

Supplies she would need to retrieve tonight, before she left the ship forever.

When Cook sent her to the hold for dinner ingredients, she knew this would be her best chance to empty her cache. The dried sausages she stuck down her hose, where they'd be hidden under her tunic. She'd lost weight while working on the ship, so her tunic hung looser than it should. That would work in her favour tonight, though, for if she cinched her belt tight around her waist, she could tuck the wineskin down the front of her tunic and no one would be any the wiser. A small, cloth-wrapped cheese made up the rest of her supplies, which were already heavier than she was used to. Sativa was tempted to leave the wine, but unless she could replace it with coin, it might be the only thing of value she could trade when she got ashore. So, the wine stayed, curved against her belly as the leather warmed until it felt like part of her own skin.

She collected what Cook had asked for and lugged the lot up the ladder to the galley, where she could hear the captain roaring accusations at his crew.

He'd discovered the missing sausages, Sativa realised with a sinking heart. And he intended to keep haranguing them until the culprit came forward, when they'd all have to watch his punishment. Sativa muttered, "I shall be back. I think I dropped something," to Cook before she fled below decks.

Instinct told her to run and hide, but Sativa ignored it. She would run, yes, but not to somewhere aboard the *Barbe*. No, it was time to go, and now would be the best time to smuggle Nekane out of the captain's cabin, while he was busy.

Remembering the darkness last time, she took a lantern with her to the cabin. She set it on the floor as she worked the bolt open, then pushed open the door.

If the captain knew she was here…she didn't know what he would do. But by the time he found out, she and Nekane would be well away.

She stepped inside the room, holding her breath as she edged around the furnishings she could barely discern in the dim light filtering through the partially open door. "Nekane?" she whispered.

No answer.

What she really needed was the lantern that she'd left outside.

Swearing inwardly at her own stupidity, Sativa turned to retrieve it.

Just in time to see the door click shut, enveloping her in darkness.

Twenty

"Where is she? Spit it out, man!" Reidar said.

Sir Edwin ducked his head. "I cannot say, Your Majesty. Nor can King Boreslas, her father. I went to Kasmirus, as you commanded, and told him I was there to escort your bride home to you. For a week, he treated me as an honoured guest, holding feasts and hunting parties, while I waited for him to produce the girl. It wasn't he who told me, but some of his courtiers, that the girl was missing. She'd disappeared on the night of the huge celebration they held for the defeat of their dragon. The king sent men all over the kingdom, looking for her, but they've found nothing. She just disappeared." He looked like he wanted to continue, but closed his mouth.

Reidar was having none of it. "What are you not telling me, Edwin?"

Edwin seemed to struggle for a moment, before he relented. "There were tales, each more fantastical than the last. Some said they'd seen the princess marry the dragonslayer, some lord or other. But he's married to some lady from Queen Margareta's court, so that cannot be true. Others say her fairy godmother whisked her away, but no one has seen a fairy godmother in the city since the girl's christening. Some say she was kidnapped, but no one saw anything. The girl has lived all her life within the castle walls — sheltered, cared for, wanting for nothing. She had no reason to run away, and yet that is the excuse the king himself gave when he finally admitted she was gone. That or she was kidnapped."

The girl he'd known would not have run away from anything. Yet how could a girl be kidnapped from her own castle without anyone seeing it happen? "Someone must have seen something," Reidar growled. He leaped to his feet and prowled behind his seat, unable to sit still.

"Perhaps they did, Your Majesty, but you must understand…" Edwin coughed. "The whole city was drunk, sire. Celebrating. They had lived in terror of the dragon for years. It devoured all of the king's other daughters. Terrorised the countryside. And then a man brought the king the beast's head. Wine and ale ran like water that night. No one remembers what they did, let alone anyone else. They are not so different from us, truly. It was like one of our grandest victory feasts. The dragon could have come back to life and whisked away the princess, and no one would have noticed a thing!"

Reidar would like to think his men would have lifted their swords to defend the girl, no matter how much ale they'd consumed. "Someone has seen her, and someone must know where she is," he said, slowing his pacing. "Offer a reward for information about her whereabouts. More if they can bring her here safely. Unharmed."

Edwin raised despairing eyes to meet Reidar's gaze. "Her father already has. He has heard nothing. He fears she may be dead, like her sisters."

No. Reidar would not believe it. His bride was alive, and she would be found. "Find her, Edwin," he said finally. "Take what ships you need, and scour the coast. Bring her to me alive, and I will shower you in riches. And if she is not…" He swallowed, not wanting to allow the thought into his head. "If she no longer lives, bring me what remains of her body. I will still reward you, but it will be with a heavy heart."

"And if I cannot? What if the girl's body lies in the depths of the sea, or in the belly of some beast? Or what if she does not wish to be found?"

Reidar sighed, suddenly tired. "Just find her, Edwin." What sort of madness had infected the man? Of course she wanted to be found.

Twenty-One

Sativa's breath caught in her throat. Perhaps someone had seen the door open, and simply pushed it shut. She would have heard if someone had come in, because if anyone found her…

Light burst upon her, an unshuttered lantern that to her dark-adjusted eyes appeared brighter than the sun.

"They say there is a hell made for the inquisitive, and they surely have a place for you, girl," a male voice said.

Sativa blinked away her blindness, then wished she hadn't. Captain Zydrunas stood before the closed door, holding her lantern high.

"The door was open, and I went to close it, but it smelled musty in here, so I thought I might tidy the place a little…" Sativa began, then trailed off. There was an unpleasant smell in the cabin. Not musty so much as rotten. Like decaying meat.

"What part of forbidden do you not understand?" the captain asked.

Sativa reddened. "I heard a woman call for help, sir, and my father told me an honourable man should help a lady in need."

The captain laughed. "You are a terrible liar, but it does not matter."

Sativa refused to back down. "I did hear a woman call for help." Not tonight, but before. Why was Nekane so silent now?

"You did not, but before this night is over, you will," the captain said, his teeth gleaming in the lamplight.

Sativa's thoughts raced. If she could get the captain away from the door, then perhaps she could get out, run up the ladder, and dive over the side into the water. She could swim to shore. She just had to make it to the water. And get the captain to move. "Then let her speak now."

Sativa hoped he would cross the room and reveal where he'd hidden Nekane. She must be gagged or unconscious, to be so silent. Sativa wouldn't be silent if there was even a slim chance of there being help at hand.

"You mean the lady from your ship? She will never speak again." The captain extended his arm and pointed.

Sativa glanced at the bunk. For a moment, she did not understand what she saw in the grey shadows. Then she realised what she saw was no shadow, lying upon the red coverlet, but a corpse. Naked and bloated, Nekane's skin had turned grey.

Sativa fought the bile rising up in her throat. This was the source of the smell. She'd been dead for days. A week or more, surely. A week in which the captain had…had…

The bile won.

Twenty-Two

"Your mother still hates me," Rudolf announced as he strode into Reidar's solar.

Reidar set down his quill. "What are you doing here? Isn't there a war you're supposed to be fighting?"

Rudolf shrugged, then stretched out on the bench beneath the window, sitting in the only patch of sun. The cat whose seat he'd usurped hissed at him, then trotted off.

"It seems word has spread among your neighbours that your throne is not worth the price they will pay to get it. That, or they are running out of men to send against us. The last two war bands we encountered took to their heels and ran away. Like rabbits!" He laughed.

"That still doesn't answer my question. Why are you here?"

"Your men can chase rabbits for a few days without me. I came to find out why you didn't send the ale you promised. Did the wedding guests drink it all, or did you just forget about us?" Rudolf sat up and peered into the corners of the room. "And where is your lovely bride? Or has she locked herself in her room, terrified after spending her wedding night with your mighty cock?"

Bawdy jokes about Sativa sat ill with Reidar. "She has not yet arrived."

Rudolf only laughed harder. "So she's heard tales about your cock and fled in fear before you can stick it in her?"

Reidar reddened. "I do not know what she's heard. I haven't seen her since she was a child. Do not jest about my bride, cousin. I warn you." Doubt gnawed at him for the first time. Crudity aside, had she heard something about him that would make her not want the marriage any more? Not want him?

"Consider me warned. You used to like jokes, Reidar. Has kingship turned you so serious that you can no longer laugh?" Concern wrinkled Rudolf's brow, all traces of humour gone.

"Not about Sativa, no. She has disappeared from her father's court, and no one has seen her since. He's sent search parties. I've sent search parties. I've even offered a reward for her safe return. She has simply vanished, as though some foul sorcery is at work betwixt her kingdom and mine." Reidar released a weighty sigh. "And while I worry for her wellbeing, my mother reminds me hourly that I need an heir. I think she has paraded every highborn girl in the kingdom before me, and quite a few not so highborn, too. More than anything, she wants me to wed. The longer Sativa is missing, the more I begin to think she might be right. Maybe I need an heir more than an alliance with Boreslas."

"Kings break betrothals every day, and alliances, too. What is so special about this girl that you cannot?"

Reidar eyed his cousin. Would the man think him weak if he confessed the truth? No one else knew. Time to test his cousin's loyalty. "In truth, I do not know. I made promises as a child, and so did she. I am loath to break my word, for what honour is there in that? I might not have seen her in years, but I have dreamed of her more nights than I can count. Not the child I knew then, but as though I watched her. She learned to ride like she was born to the saddle, and hunted with her father's court before she could lift a bow. She never made a kill, but she loved the chase. She would teach her sisters, teaching them to write so they might manage kingdoms of their own, when they were queens in their own right. And lately, I have dreamed of her flying through the air at a great height. Ships below her, or sometimes the sea. She's not an angel, but…it's like nothing I can explain. I know she lives, and she is coming to me. For weeks I have known this, and still she is not here!"

Rudolf nodded slowly. "There is some magic at work, then. A bond between you that perhaps only death can break. Tell me, what does this girl of yours look like?"

"As fair as the sun," Reidar replied. "No matter how many other girls my mother places before me, the only face I see is hers. A face I do not know!"

"You have it bad, cousin. I hope she is worth the wait. And, in a similar vein, I have a confession to make, too."

Reidar raised an eyebrow. "Oh?"

Rudolf's smile was rueful. "Will you ever release me to return to the Southern Isles?"

"You don't want to be king?" Reidar blurted out.

Rudolf laughed softly. "I never said that. I asked if you would let me go home."

Reidar wasn't sure what to say. "But you are

my heir. Until I have a son, that is. And there is this war..."

"The war will never be over, but your neighbours will learn, and so will your own men. There are leaders among them, and they are loyal to you. There will come a time when you don't need me. You will choose a bride – whether your betrothed or some other girl – and there will be children to take your place. When that time comes, I ask you to let me return home."

There was no laughter in Rudolf's eyes now. Only pain.

"Why?" Reidar asked hoarsely.

"Like you, I dream of a girl. A woman, now. I made promises, which I intend to keep." Rudolf smiled sadly. "Oh, not like you. There is no betrothal between us. But yours is not the only war – and other kings have seen the richness of the Southern Isles, wishing to conquer them for their own. There are many lords of the islands, and some call themselves kings, but they recognise one man as their leader, and he has no sons. Only daughters."

Now Reidar understood. "You want to be king of the Southern Isles, and take one of the daughters for your queen." A king in his own right. "But the Southern Isles still belong to Viken."

"Not for long, if the other kings have their way. I mean to take a small force and together with the men of the isles, claim them for my own. I will still bend the knee to you, of course, but without someone to lead them, the isles will fall." Rudolf clenched his hands into fists. "I will not let that happen."

"What is there about these isles that inspires such passion?" Reidar asked.

Rudolf coughed. "My passion is not for the isles, but for the lady. The isles are her birthright."

Winning lands a world away for the love of a woman. Well. Reidar had never expected this.

"When my wife gives birth to a son, you are free to return," Reidar said. "I'm sure you will find men here willing to flock to your cause, if only for the adventure of a trip to the Southern Isles. But do not take too many, for I will not lose the war here so you can have your woman!"

Rudolf bowed low. "As Your Majesty commands."

"Is she fair, this lady?" Reidar asked, unable to resist.

"Her skin is fair, but her hair reminds me of a bonfire blaze. Portia is like no lady I have ever met." It was Rudolf's turn to sigh, as his eyes turned to the south-west.

Reidar laughed. "What a pair we are, mooning after girls who are not yet our wives. But, God willing, they will be. What will we do while we wait for the time to be right?"

Rudolf shrugged. "What men always do, I suppose. Make war. Make merry. Make our mothers despair of us ever growing up."

Reidar clapped his cousin on the back. "Sounds like a fine plan. I have another. We have not celebrated your return yet, and

Mother is always pestering me to hold another feast. She wants only to parade more maidens before me, of course, but what of it? It is many months since I have gone hunting, and the boars are fat this time of year. Let's put together a hunting party on the morrow, and on our return, there shall be a welcome feast in your honour."

"I have not tasted Viken boar since I left your shores, and the pigs in the Southern Isles cannot compare. Let us forget women and the worries of your kingdom for a few days, and enjoy the hunt!" Rudolf grinned. "Thank you, cousin. It is good to be back."

It was good to have him back, Reidar thought. Now all he needed was Sativa, and he could be happy.

Twenty-Three

Sativa wiped her mouth with the back of her hand. Her mother would despair if she knew, but Sativa had no handkerchief here.

"Why?" she whispered.

Captain Zydrunas shrugged. "Like most women, she was too noisy for her own good. Inquisitive. Complaining. And tears…ugh." He shuddered.

An arrow of remorse shot through Sativa's heart. She had disliked Nekane's constant tears and mourning, too, but she'd never wanted to kill her. She was a widow, and widows were allowed to weep.

"You are a monster," Sativa said. It was a calm statement of fact.

Why wouldn't he move away from the door? she raged inwardly.

"All men are monsters in their own way," he said loftily. He nodded at Nekane, and there was considerable pride in his voice as he added, "She said I was like a dragon."

"It was no compliment," Sativa shot back. "Dragons are mindless beasts, who don't know the difference between a sheep and a woman in wool. They burn and devour because they don't know any better. Men are more than that."

At least, the men in her father's court had been. Those aboard the *Wydra*. And Reidar.

"I would take a dragon over you any day," she added, more to bait him than anything else.

It worked. He moved away from the door, but only to approach her. "But you will take me, girl. She could not stop me, and nor will you."

He would kill her, and defile her dead body. Horror made her jaw drop, but some other instinct told her to draw her dagger. She did.

Zydrunas set the lantern on the table, and drew his own knife. Easily thrice as long as hers, the steel blade seemed to drink the light instead of reflecting it. He thrust across the table, and Sativa barely managed to dodge the wicked point. Her arm seemed to have a life of its own, driving down to slice his hand.

Zydrunas swore. "Little bitch. I was going to cut your throat, nice and easy, but you'll have no quick death from me now. You shall suffer."

Faster than Sativa believed possible, he whipped his blade to the side, slashing it across her belly. Warm liquid gushed out, soaking her tunic, but the wound came with no pain. Sativa pressed her hands to her belly, and they came away red. She turned horrified eyes on the captain as she backed away.

He made no move to follow her now. He

knew as well as she did that she was as good as dead.

Instead, he crossed to the bed. He lifted Nekane's corpse in his arms, and she flopped like some obscene rag doll as he carried her over to the bench Sativa recognised as a privy. He kicked open the lid and forced the body in, feet first. He managed to get her halfway in, before she stuck, her torso sticking out of the privy like a giant glove puppet.

"She can watch you die, then," he said, forcing the corpse's eyes open. Gore dribbled down Nekane's bloated face — there was nothing recognisable about her eyes any more. The widow was with her husband, now.

Doubled over in the corner, one arm pressed to her belly, Sativa still pointed the knife at him, but for how long, she wasn't sure. "You deserve to die," she hissed.

He laughed. "Not today. Today, I get a new bride in my bed." He crossed to the door and yanked it open. "I will return when you are finished fighting, but still warm." And out he went, closing the door behind him. He drove the bolt home, a final nail in Sativa's coffin.

She collapsed on the floor, spent. What was there left to fight for, now? Not even she could fight death.

Twenty-Four

"There is a particularly fine beast I've seen in the southern woods, sire," one of the woodsmen said. "Powerful fierce, like he's possessed by some devilish spirit. We stay in the northern parts while he's about."

Reidar nodded. They couldn't have brought him better news. "Just the sort of challenge I'd like," he said, tossing a purse of coin at the man's feet. "Stay out of the forest for a few days, while we hunt. You will know when the beast is caught, for there will be a feast at the castle."

Both men bowed. "Thank you, sire. We will."

Reidar had given them enough money to feed two families for a week, or perhaps a little more. Surely that would be long enough. A week free of the cares of his kingdom, or worry for Sativa. Bliss, surely.

He called to his men, and the spearbearers, to follow him into the forest.

A quick fight, a bit of spilled blood, and victory to follow. Truly the sport of kings.

He kicked his horse into a gallop, and set off between the trees.

Twenty-Five

He'd left the lantern to taunt her, Sativa was sure of it. There was not even a window to look or squeeze out of – no exit but the bolted door. Her only escape was death, like poor Nekane.

Who was still stuck in the privy, poor woman.

Sativa's hands were sticky and red, and her tunic and hose were soaked. She hadn't known a body could lose this much blood and still live. And yet…still she felt no pain.

Did that mean she was near the end? The end where the devil of a captain would do things to her corpse?

Never.

There had to be a way out.

She glanced at Nekane. Perhaps the dead widow did hold the answer.

As Sativa approached her, the stench grew, until she had to haul her tunic over her nose to bear it. This was the smell of death, though, and not the privy beneath her. And if it was anything like the privy aboard the *Wydra*, it let out into the water.

Sativa swallowed, took hold of the corpse's shoulders, and shoved. No, the body was stuck. She studied it for a moment, then realised why. Gingerly, she pried the woman's arms out of the hole and lifted them. The body slid so fast it almost took her with it, but Sativa grabbed onto the lip of the privy in time to save herself.

Save herself from what? A watery death was better than what waited for her here.

Something tumbled from her tunic, and she instinctively reached to catch it before it fell. Too late, she realised she could be grasping for her own innards, and drew her hand back.

To her surprise, a slashed wineskin dropped into the privy, landing in the darkness with a splash.

A slashed…but the wineskin had been full. Sativa fumbled at her soaked tunic, trying to undo her belt to see the skin underneath, and the wound that should be there. The one that would kill her. The wound that…

…wasn't there.

The stupid captain had stabbed the wineskin instead. But he'd soon be back, to do horrible things to her still-warm corpse. More than ever, she needed to get out.

She eyed the privy. It was the only way.

Sativa perched on the edge, uttering a prayer that she might reach shore safely. And not get stuck.

She took a deep breath, and let go.

Twenty-Six

The day ended without anyone sighting the boar, but Reidar was content. There'd been signs of the beast, and they were certainly in its territory now.

He shared a cup of ale with Rudolf by the fire as servants pitched his pavilion and prepared their meal.

"You should have seen your face. You were so certain you'd found the beast in the bushes, and that it would be your kill, when all the rest of us said we were too far north. Standing there like some ancient colossus…and out popped…a squirrel!" Reidar roared with laughter.

Rudolf didn't seem to find it as funny, though he did laugh. "You always were the better hunter. I left before I was old enough to join your father's hunting parties. It sounded big enough to be a boar!"

"Rudolph the great squirrel slayer!" Reidar howled. He laughed until his belly ached. He had not felt this free in years.

"Tomorrow will be better," Rudolf said. "You may take the beast, and when you miss, then I'll take my shot."

Reidar spat out his ale. "I do not miss!"

Rudolf smiled. "We shall see, cousin. We shall see."

The evening was a merry one, with plenty of ale and even a little singing around the fire, until someone reminded them all that singing would only drive the beast away, not bring it within range of their spears. They quietened after that.

When they retired for the night, Reidar felt an inexplicable chill. No one else seemed to notice, so he merely called for some extra furs and told himself that would be an end to it.

The cold seemed to have settled in his bones, and it took some time to dispel, but eventually he forgot he was in the forest and may as well have been in his chamber at home, he was so warm.

Rudolf was right. Tomorrow would be better. A sense of wellbeing washed over him, like he'd been engulfed by one of the waves he could hear crashing on the not-too-distant shore, and he drifted off into a dream where Sativa sat at his side instead of his cousin, and after they shared a cup of ale, they shared a kiss. The kiss lasted until he carried her to his bedroll and their night together was bliss. Oh, what a dream.

If only it were true.

Twenty-Seven

Sativa gasped as the freezing water engulfed her, her last breath before the sea closed over her head. She kicked off the side of the ship, heading for the wavering light at what she thought was the surface. She burst into cold air and wished she hadn't, as the breeze turned out to be colder than the water.

Dusk had fallen, but there was enough light to see the darkness that was the shore. Praying that no one aboard the ship saw her, she set out for land.

Her hose and boots drank seawater like a drowning man, weighing her down. Determined not to drown when she was so close to her destination, Sativa stripped off the offending items. Only modesty made her keep her tunic. That and the camouflage it offered her pale skin as the moon rose.

An eternity passed, as she stroked for shore. Kicking, pulling with her arms, taking breath after breath and spitting out salt water as the waves taunted her, but the beach drew ever closer.

Then a wave picked her up and her arms windmilled wildly as she tried to paddle out of it, but to no avail. The wave broke, plunging her beneath the water until she grazed the sandy seabed. Gasping, Sativa kicked off the bottom, only to find that her head broke the surface before her feet had left the seafloor. She staggered ashore, barely believing she'd made it. She wanted to lie on the sand and sleep for a week, but she couldn't. Not while she was still so close to the ship. Still visible to them, perhaps.

Her legs felt like they carried their own ballast, they were so heavy, as she dragged herself up the beach and into the trees. A breath of wind was enough to send her teeth chattering as her bones turned to solid ice. Still she trudged on. There would be no wind once she was deep enough into the forest.

A few steps in, then a few more. Soon, she could no longer see the beach, but she could hear the waves. Still she walked. She would continue until she couldn't any more, and then she would lie down and sleep.

Moonlight was dim between the trees, so she stumbled often, but Sativa refused to stop. It looked like it was growing lighter ahead. Light could only mean people, and civilisation. Someone who could help her.

A large fire sat in the clearing, sending up a prayer of smoke into the sky. Sativa thanked whoever had lit it, and approached as close as she dared, holding out her hands to warm them. She had nothing left to trade but the small cheese, wrapped in its now salt-stained cloth, but she would offer it gladly if it meant getting warm and dry again.

"You kept me waiting," a grumpy voice greeted her. Oh, the voice was old and scratchy, too, but the elderly woman wanted her irritation known.

"Please forgive me," Sativa said politely. She had heard that old women who lived too long sometimes lost their wits, and she had been taught to be polite to her elders.

A hunched figure stepped out of the shadows and straightened. "Your father taught you well, Princess."

Sativa squinted at the woman. "Do I know you?"

The woman cackled, then coughed. "Perhaps, perhaps not. I am too old to be your fairy godmother, in truth, but as my daughter is still learning to take my place, I wanted to see you one last time. I am Dalia."

Though the hem of her tunic was too short to do it properly, Sativa attempted a respectful curtsey. "I am honoured, Godmother Dalia."

"Come, girl. My visions said you would be hungry, and in need of a fire's warmth. You are not out of the woods yet."

Sativa did as her godmother bade her. For the first time in she couldn't remember how long, she ate her fill, and the food was good. But the wine was too strong, and she began to wish that she had not drunk so much of it, for her eyes started to close of their own accord.

Sativa blinked back drowsiness, wanting to ask the question that burned in her mind before she surrendered to sleep. "Godmother Dalia, thank you for your hospitality. I am grateful but…I must know one thing."

Dalia grinned, her eyes seeming to glow in the firelight. "Yes?"

Sativa fought to find the words that wouldn't make her question sound like an accusation. "Why are you here now? Why not earlier, when I was kidnapped by pirates, or locked in that room, or earlier still, when my father tried to marry me to a shoemaker?"

Dalia nodded. "Do you know what my powers are?"

"You are a seer," Sativa said. "I do not know what else."

"I sometimes see the future, yes, as I foresaw your sisters would die because of a creature that came out of the darkness, as a different darkness would swallow you, too, in time. I have a talent for curses, or I did. It's been many years since I cast one."

"So you saw the pirates, and the shoemaker, and everything else?" Sativa asked impatiently.

Dalia nodded once more. "I saw the pirates, and much of your flight from your father's court. Yes. The shoemaker…ah, young George's fate has little to do with yours. He was always destined for Melitta. He's my daughter's godson, you know."

Sativa's head hurt. There was so much she didn't understand. "But why are you here?"

Dalia blinked. "Because you need me, of course! If I weren't here, you'd freeze your little titties off in the forest and never find your way to that handsome king of yours."

King? "Reidar is a prince, not a king."

"When his father died, your Prince Reidar became king. He's eager for a queen, though, so you mustn't delay. Tonight, you may rest, but in the morning, you must find him."

Sativa couldn't seem to stay upright any more. Too tired. Her head rested on the ground and it was too comfortable to resist. "Will you show me the way?" she mumbled.

"No, dear, I'm too old to be traipsing around the forest. My friend will show you the way. As long as you follow her, you won't get lost."

"Oh, good," Sativa tried to say but she wasn't sure if she managed to get the words out before she fell asleep.

Twenty-Eight

A shaft of sunlight tickled Sativa's eyelids as it passed. She pulled her blankets more closely about her, wondering why her chamber was so cold. The fire must have gone out in the night, or someone had left the shutters open. Probably her sister Stella, who liked to look up at the stars.

No, Stella was dead, devoured by a dragon, like the rest of her sisters. And Sativa could not be in her chambers, for she slept aboard a pirate ship, pretending to be a boy until the ship came close enough to shore to swim to safety.

Ugh. Swimming. Fighting the waves until they grew tired of her feeble flailing and flung her on the shore.

Now she remembered the night that had been. Or had it been a dream? Nekane, the crazy captain, and her future-seeing fairy godmother?

Sativa blinked her eyes open.

Last night's great bonfire had burned down to coals, and her one thin blanket did little to keep out the early morning chill.

"Mrow?"

Sativa stared in surprise at the source of the sound. A cat the colour of smoke sat beside the fire, licking at a package Sativa recognised — the cheese she'd stolen from the *Barbe*. The only food she had.

Sativa scrambled to her feet and attempted to shoo the animal away, but it only turned to hiss at her before returning to what was left of its meal. Precious little, she found, when she ventured close enough to see. No point in wasting her time for a bite or two of drowned cheese.

When the cat was finished eating, it sat to wash its fluffy fur, taking its time in a grooming ritual that could have satisfied a palace lap-cat, instead of this forest-born beast. When the beast's bath was done, it crossed the clearing and stopped to look back at Sativa. "Mrow?"

She shook her head at the expectant beast. "No. Dalia said to wait here for her friend, who would guide me."

"Mrow." Was it possible for a cat to look exasperated, or was Sativa simply imagining the expression on the cat's face?

She regarded the cat for a long moment. "I don't suppose you're a female cat? Dalia did say her friend was female, though surely she would have told me if she was feline, too."

"Mrow."

Sativa sighed. Try as she might, she'd never understand the cat's meaning. Being able to talk to beasts would be a useful gift around about now. If she was wrong about this…

Reluctantly, she dropped her blanket on the ground, shaping it into an arrowhead that pointed in the cat's direction. The direction she would follow the beast, though it might be folly, and the way Dalia's friend would have to go in order to find her if the cat was not the promised guide.

Swearing roundly at all the sharp sticks on the forest floor and herself for losing her boots in the sea, Sativa set off behind the cat.

Twenty-Nine

Reidar sat by the rekindled fire, a crust of bread in one hand and a cup of ale in the other as he broke his fast, while the rest of the hunting party readied themselves for the day. His pavilion was already packed away, but others were not as used to travelling as he and several tents still stood in the clearing.

Einar strutted around without his tunic, pointing at the scars on his chest that were hard to see beneath all the white hair, and telling the tales of how he got them to any man who'd listen, and quite a few who didn't.

Dag had brought a hound that he swore could sniff out boars better than any beast alive, and he had a leash around its neck, letting it lead him around the clearing, sniffing for signs for their quarry. So far, it had found and frightened two squirrels, twice Rudolf's score from yesterday.

Rudolf emerged from the trees, straightening his tunic. Another man who had to piss away a lot of last night's ale.

Reidar nodded at Dag and his dog. "What do you say, cousin? Shall we let the beast lead the way today?"

Rudolf shrugged.

"He has a scent! Sire, we should follow it!" Dag shouted.

Others caught his excitement and headed for their horses.

Reidar rose. "Why not? Let's ride. I fancy roast pork for my dinner."

Rudolf was close behind him. "A wager, cousin? That you will take home your heart's desire today?"

Reidar turned to stare at Rudolf. Such a strange thing to say. Almost as though the man knew what he'd dreamed last night. "There is no wager to make. I smell victory in the air today."

Behind him, Rudolf's voice said softly, in a tone so low Reidar suspected he wasn't supposed to hear: "We shall see. Stranger things have happened to kings while hunting. I suspect victory will not be yours on this day."

A chill closed around Reidar's heart, but he shook it off. Rudolf's words could be traitorous or prophetic, or mere nonsense he'd spouted to make mischief. Whatever the truth, it would out itself today, for one thing was certain — there was something different in the air. An expectation, a promise…of change. And he would embrace it.

Reidar leaped onto his horse's back. "Time for the hunt to begin!" he shouted.

And so it began.

Thirty

The damned cat was like water — endlessly running, while Sativa struggled to keep up. When Sativa stopped to rest or take a drink before crossing yet another stream, the animal would sit and stare at her, occasionally uttering that same, superior, "Mrow," that seemed to be all it could say.

Her feet hurt. No, all of her body hurt, and her belly added an extra growled protest at the absence of breakfast. In the tales she'd heard as a child, there were berries and all sorts of things to eat in the forest. So far, she'd seen nothing except her stolen cheese. The one the cat had eaten. Idly, she wondered if cats were edible.

As though the beast had heard her, the cat stopped, then scrambled up a tree.

Annoyed, Sativa stumbled to the trunk and peered up. "I can climb, too, you know."

Something exploded out of the underbrush behind her, setting the squirrels chittering away in fear.

Sativa risked a glance over her shoulder and almost screamed at the biggest tusked pig she'd ever seen, mere yards from her.

The beast hadn't noticed her yet, but if it did, one of those tusks could end her as surely as Captain Zydrunas' blade, and she had no skin of wine to save her now.

Sativa leaped, reaching for the nearest branch as her feet scrabbled for purchase on the tree trunk. Her muscles screamed as she climbed, but she knew she'd scream louder if the pig got to her.

Her bare feet slipped, leaving her hanging in the air a few inches from the ground.

The pig turned, and its small eyes seemed to glow red as it spied Sativa. The beast charged.

Her arms ached from trying to support her whole weight, but Sativa did her best to swing her body to the side in one last, desperate hope that she might gain a foothold on the slippery tree.

She managed to get out of the way of the pig's charge, but then it crashed into the tree. Hard. She lost her grip and came tumbling down on top of the animal's bristled back.

Instinctively, she hung on, but the rampaging pig was no tree. Still, she knew if she fell, it would trample her to death if it didn't gore her first. Yet she stayed on, and it took her a moment to realise why.

When the pig had hit the tree, its tusks had gotten stuck. It seemed more concerned at getting free of the tree than bucking her off.

She could climb off and run, but where would she go? Could she climb a different tree before the beast fought itself free?

Hadn't the shoemaker told a tale of how he'd slayed a boar by getting it stuck in a tree?

Before she could answer her own questions, the cat intervened.

As nimble as any sailor, it ran down the tree trunk, jumped on the pig's head, then used it as a springboard to leap away into the forest.

And in so doing, freed the beast's tusks.

Summoning some vague memory from the shoemaker's tales, Sativa yanked out her knife and plunged it into the beast's throat. Once, twice, before the squealing animal threw her off.

Sativa landed heavily on her back, but she leaped to her feet, ready to run.

But the pig didn't seem to see her any more as it danced around in a frenzy, trying to dislodge the knife in its throat as its lifeblood flowed out onto the forest floor.

Finally, it collapsed in a heap, sides heaving, as it turned baleful eyes on Sativa once more.

Fury forced her to hold her ground. "After

surviving pirates, I'm not about to surrender to a pig," she said.

The beast seemed to understand. It took one last breath, and then stilled.

Sativa waited for a long moment before she dared approach. She nudged the animal with her foot, but it didn't move. Only then did she lean down to retrieve her knife. The handle was slick with blood, and it took her a few tries to pull it out. She succeeded on the fourth attempt, only to have a gush of blood spatter her with gore.

Sativa glanced down. Between the wine stains and the blood, she didn't think Melitta would want her torn tunic back.

Her belly growled in agreement.

Sativa wanted to laugh. How she could still be hungry while looking at the bloody pig, she wasn't sure, but it was a pig. Pigs meant pork and bacon and ham and all sorts of things that would make a lovely breakfast. She'd have to butcher it first and work out how to cook it, but just the thought of roast pork made her willing to try.

Hooves thudded behind her. Lots of them.

Fearing the pig's herd had come to seek their revenge, Sativa whirled, knife in one hand, and murder in her eyes.

Thirty-One

"This way!" Dag cried, urging his horse after the dog.

Reidar had long since come to believe there was no pig at all, a thought some of the others had muttered aloud, but he was loath to call off a chase when he was enjoying himself. So he followed Dag and the others followed after.

The dog went mad, almost dragging the leash out of Dag's hand. Dag's horse reared back, and the man had a good deal of trouble getting both beasts under control. In the confusion, Rudolf moved ahead.

"What's the beast found this time?" Reidar asked. "Another squirrel, perhaps?"

The others laughed. All but Rudolf.

Rudolf was strangely silent for a long moment, before he said, "The hound has found a pig, all right, and more besides."

"What do you mean?" Reidar said.

Rudolf beckoned, riding forward.

Reidar followed.

Thirty-Two

Not pigs, but men on horseback. Lots of them, armed and dressed like the warriors they were. They crowded into the clearing, and yet they held back, keeping their horses away from the pig carcass.

The girl she had been would have dropped the dagger and begged for help, but Sativa had not journeyed across the sea for nothing. She'd bury the blade in her own breast before letting any of these men touch her. So she brandished her knife and held her ground.

"There's your pig, cousin," one man said. "It seems the victor on the field is a girl today."

Laughter bubbled up from the other men.

"I'll thank you to keep your covetous hands off my pig," Sativa snapped. Her fury blazed bigger than the bonfire last night.

"This is the king's forest, his private hunting preserve, and he alone owns everything in it. Including that pig," the first man said calmly.

Sativa thought for a moment. She'd heard similar things at home, but there was more to it than that. "The beast charged at me. Tried to kill me. I vanquished my foe, which makes everything he owns forfeit to me. The pig might only have meat, but the meat is mine!"

Laughter died as the men surveyed the scene. The blood, the pig, the dagger in her hand. Lust began to smoulder in their eyes.

One man pushed forward, while the rest hung back. He stared hungrily at her chest.

Sativa glanced down. Her tunic left little to the imagination, and her necklace had fallen out. Carefully, she tucked the amber ring out of sight and tried to hold the worst rip together.

This only seemed to inflame the man further. "Back away, all of you," he said softly. "She is mine."

Sativa swallowed. "The first man to touch me will die like that pig." She jerked her knife at the carcass. "I belong to no man. Not even your king. Who owes me a bite of that beast, once his cooks are done with it."

Thirty-Three

"Skadi," Rudolf breathed.

For a moment, Reidar saw what Rudolf did. The blood-spattered girl could have been a goddess from the old faith. Skadi, goddess of the hunt…but also the goddess of justice, vengeance and righteous anger.

"I belong to no man. Not even your king. Who owes me a bite of that beast, once his cooks are done with it."

Reidar laughed aloud at this girl's courage. Armed with a knife before a dozen mounted knights, she showed no fear whatsoever. But a girl who could take on a full-grown boar with nothing more than a dagger was a force to be reckoned with. A huntress indeed.

And yet…she seemed familiar somehow. Something about the proud set of her head, as she dropped neither bow nor curtsey as she met his gaze. Almost as though she considered herself his equal.

And there was that glimpse of gold, now hidden beneath her shift, that made him wonder all the more.

He slid down from his horse. "We will make camp here for the night," he announced. Reidar waited until he and the girl were alone before he added, "I will offer you a meal and a bed for the night, and on the morrow I will take you to the castle where the king lives. You can bring the pig, too, and I'll see that the castle kitchens prepare it properly. You can't ask for fairer than that."

She stared at him for a moment, as though reading his soul, then nodded. She crouched to wipe her blade on the grass before tucking it away. Only as she reached her full height once more did she fold her arms across her breasts, and Reidar realised that she must be freezing, wearing nothing but a shift.

He shrugged off his cloak and held it out. "Please take it. You must be cold."

Once again, she hesitated, before she accepted the cloak. "I thank you," she said.

He stood beside her in silence, though his curiosity burned fiercer than any fire. He had so many questions he wanted to ask that he wasn't sure which should be first.

When his servants seemed to take an inordinately long time setting up his pavilion, he decided to satisfy a tiny part of his curiosity.

"Show me what you wear around your neck," he said.

Her eyes seemed filled with fire. "What I wear around my neck is none of your business, sir."

So she did not know him, then. "What if I were to tell you that I am the king of these lands, and everything and everyone within my borders is my business?"

She sized him up. Finally, her shoulders seemed to relax and she said, "If what you say is true, then perhaps it is your business, after all." She drew a leather thong from beneath her shift, and held it up. Suspended from the cord was a silver ring with a yellow-gold stone.

A ring that would not fit on even Reidar's smallest finger, now, but he recognised it like it was yesterday.

"How did you come to have this?"

She tucked the necklace beneath her borrowed cloak. "If you are truly the king of these lands, then you already know the answer."

Sativa. Hope welled in his breast, but Reidar forced it back down. He couldn't be certain. Not yet. "This ring was given to a girl to whom I made a promise. Only she and I knew of it, though there was one other witness to my vow."

Her eyebrows rose. "There was?"

He almost laughed, but he managed to control himself. "One who is not likely to speak of it. He was the fattest pony I had ever beheld."

She laughed. "I'd forgotten about Philip. I gave him to my sisters soon after that, who spoiled him far more than I ever did. If horses ever receive a divine reward, then I hope he is reunited with them in heaven."

There was no doubt in Reidar's mind now. He'd found her, and he had no intention of letting her out of his sight until they were married.

"Sire, your tent is ready for you," a servant said, bowing low.

Reidar bowed to Sativa. "After you."

The servant looked surprised, but Reidar caught many startled glances aimed at the girl as they headed for his tent. For a moment, he saw what they did – a bedraggled girl in a torn shift, whose only protection was the king's cloak. They would look at her very differently when he crowned her as his queen. Reidar grinned.

Only Rudolf dared to put his thoughts into words. He bowed extravagantly in his cousin's direction. "I wish you a pleasurable night, Your Majesty, with such pleasant company. Your little goddess might be a beautiful woman under all the dirt." He eyed Sativa appreciatively.

"Put your eyes back in your head, man," Reidar snapped. "Don't you have a wife waiting for you on some island somewhere? This one's mine." He put a proprietary arm around Sativa and pushed her into his pavilion.

"If you are sure, cousin," Rudolf said, turning away. "My best wishes for your health and happiness, then."

Happiness. Yes. Reidar's smile returned, and he stepped into his tent.

Only to meet the point of Sativa's blade, aimed between his eyes.

"If you think I will allow you to kill me and rape my corpse, you are mistaken," she said fiercely.

Reidar's mouth dropped open. It was a long moment before he managed to say, "Honestly, neither of those things have ever crossed my mind. It sounds like you have endured quite an ordeal, Princess Sativa, since you left your father's castle. He's had men scouring the country for you, but it seems he underestimated you. Yet there is one thing I don't understand. Why are you here?"

"My father offered me as a prize to any man who could slay a dragon," Sativa said. "On the night he was to have me marry a shoemaker, I remembered a prior engagement."

Reidar laughed. "In that case, I offer you my protection, and my hospitality, for as long as you wish," Reidar replied. "Even my sword, to defend you against this shoemaker, should he come searching for you."

"He will not come searching for me. His heart lies elsewhere."

Reidar spread his arms wide. "Then what do you wish of me? If it is within my power, I will grant it, Princess."

For the second time, she tucked her knife away. Reidar hoped it would be the last, for this being threatened by women with weapons would take some getting used to.

"Years ago, you talked of a tower," she began cautiously.

Hope blossomed within him. "I promised a tower and a crown, to the woman who would become my queen," Reidar corrected.

For the first time, she smiled. "I'd settle for some water to wash with and a bed, then maybe a meal and something to wear that isn't covered in blood."

Reidar wanted to envelop her in his arms and swear to take care of her for the rest of her days. What had the girl been through to get here? Killing a boar with nothing but a knife. He couldn't have done it. Half foreign princess, half ancient goddess come to life, and every inch the woman of his dreams.

But her eyes were wary, as well they might be, for she did not know him yet.

"It will be as you command, Princess," he

said.

She lifted her chin. "I do."

Thirty-Four

As Sativa settled into the king's bed – without the king, for Reidar slept outside the tent, as he insisted her honour demanded – she let out a sigh of contentment. She'd washed away weeks' worth of salt and dirt as best she could with just a cloth and basin of water. She'd eaten a meal worth tasting for the first time in weeks. And she now wore a tunic without holes, as fine as Melitta's had once been before time and trouble had worn it to rags.

She was safe. Whatever happened next was

for Reidar to worry about, not her. No more pirates or perilous voyages or pea straw or pigs. Ever again.

She remembered the lust in his eyes, not unlike the look every man wore when he looked at a beautiful woman. What would it feel like to surrender to such a thing? Not the cruel hands of a man like Zydrunas, but the welcoming arms of Reidar. A king who could take what he wanted without asking, and yet he held back for honour's sake, or so he said.

He'd offered her his own cloak, his bed, his…everything. She'd crossed the seas to accept a man she barely knew, but she'd dreamed of for as long as she could remember. Could the dream match the reality?

His hands as he'd laid the cloak on her shoulders, wrapping its folds around her, still warm from his body. Strong and gentle, all at the same time. And reverent, too.

The look on his face as he'd brought her food. Not a servant – he'd carried the platter with his own hands, and shared it with her, for he'd brought enough for two. He'd pointed out the choicest morsels and insisted they were hers. The lust was gone, as though it had never been, replaced with tenderness. Did she imagine a little longing, too? Probably. But alone in her bed, nay, his bed, she let herself believe it. That Reidar longed for her the way she did for him.

Thoughts of him warmed her through the night, and in the cold morning, as well, as she mounted up behind Reidar for the ride back to the castle. At first, the heat of him between her thighs made her blush, but that was what she'd come for, hadn't she? To be his wife, to share his bed and his body and all that he could give her. So she held her head high, wrapped her arms around his hard torso, and hung on to the man who would be her husband.

All too soon, the forest gave way to farmland, and a castle appeared on the cliffs. Smaller than her father's, but above it loomed the most delightful sight of all — the Sea Tower, Reidar's promise.

"Thank you," she whispered, pressing her lips to his neck. "Thank you."

He reached back and cradled her head in his hand, as though he wanted to prolong the kiss. "I am a man of my word, Princess. I promise you that."

Not a princess for much longer. She had promised to be his queen, and Sativa would keep her word, as he'd kept his.

When they rode through the gate of her king's castle, Sativa couldn't suppress a smile as she surveyed her new home.

Thirty-Five

The warm woman at his back set him on fire. The grin on Reidar's face didn't fade for the whole ride home. Some of the other men winked knowingly, thinking they knew what had passed between him and Sativa. He let them believe what they liked. It was no dishonour for a Viken woman to take a lover, unless she had a husband. Sativa could have chosen any one of them to spend the night with, and Reidar would have had no right to complain. It would have sat ill with him, of course, especially if she decided she liked another man more than him…

Reidar shook his head. But she had chosen him, and no other man. He'd even offered her a horse of her own to ride, but she'd refused and insisted on riding with him. He couldn't tell her how thankful he was for that — the reassuring weight of her behind him, reminding him that everything was right in the world, now that she'd been found. When she was ready and fully recovered from her ordeal, she would name a date for their wedding, and the wedding night that would follow.

Then he would do things to her he'd only dreamed of — all of last night, in fact — as he worshipped her like the goddess she'd resembled. So what if it was sacrilegious? She would be his wife, the woman he'd vowed to honour and cherish. What was worship but an elevated mixture of the two?

All too soon, their ride ended as his castle loomed into view, with her tower standing sentinel above it. Reidar wondered what she would think of a castle so much smaller than her father's. Cold, grey stone instead of warm brick, perched on a clifftop over a turbulent sea, instead of sitting comfortably on a hilltop overlooking vast fields of prosperous farmland.

"I offer you the hospitality of my home, humble though it is," Reidar said. He held his breath, praying she would accept.

Sativa's arms tightened around him as her soft lips kissed his neck. "Thank you. Thank you."

Every bit of him wanted to turn around, take her in her arms and kiss her breathless. Kiss her until he was breathless, too. Reidar realised he had his hand on her face, and he'd half turned to do what he was dreaming about. Not yet, he told himself, forcing his hand to take the reins again.

"The king has returned! The king has returned!" someone shouted from the gate, and then they all took up the cry.

It wasn't a cry of triumph. Something was

wrong.

Hakon raced across the bailey and stopped, panting, as Reidar reined in his horse. "Raiders. A whole fleet of them, spotted from the Sea Tower this morning. Headed for the port. They should reach there soon after darkness, and if they do…"

Reidar understood. "With the army near the inland borders and our ships off helping King Boreslas with the search, they'll be defenceless. We'll go at once. Send any able bodied man you can spare after me."

"You're riding to war?" Sativa's voice asked near his ear.

Oh, by all that was holy, he'd forgotten her. But he didn't have time to explain.

"I must," he said, swinging her out of the saddle and onto the ground. "I will return when the battle is won, or the port is lost." He addressed Hakon. "Take her to the queen. Tell the queen to take care of her until my return." Reidar wheeled his horse around, ready to ride out of the gate.

Rudolf blocked his path. "You can't afford to lose the port," he said bluntly.

"I know that. I'm not a fool," Reidar snapped.

"The people of the Southern Isles have been defending against sea raids for centuries, sometimes successfully. They have an idea they came up with after watching some of our funerals," Rudolf said. He grinned. "Fire arrows. They set fire to the boats before the men can come ashore. Sometimes even ambush them where they know the boats will sink and the raiders will drown. You need fire arrows, and a narrow place they will be forced to sail through where they will be in range of our archers. How many archers can we have there in time?"

Hope blossomed in Reidar's breast. "More than we need. Every man and boy between here and the port can shoot a bow, because the lake is full of geese in the summertime, and any man who can shoot a bird may take it home for his table. Maybe we can save the port after all!"

He and Rudolf rode out, discussing likely ambush sites as they went.

Thirty-Six

Everything was wonderful…and then it wasn't, as Reidar dropped her on the ground like a sack of apples and rode off with his cousin to war, without even saying farewell. Not that she would have heard it if he had, for there was another word that burned in her brain with a ferocity she wasn't sure how to tame: queen.

As in: "Take her to the queen."

Wasn't she supposed to be his queen? His betrothed, his bride, the woman he would marry?

But if he already had a queen…it would explain why he hadn't even suggested sharing her bed. Why he hadn't mentioned marriage or their betrothal in the forest.

And why someone had seen the ships from the top of the tower – someone else already lived there.

Reidar's servant bade her to follow him and she did, but she paid little attention to her surroundings. For the first time, she wondered if she'd made a terrible mistake in coming here. If she wasn't wanted…

"Forgive me, Your Majesty, but the king said I must bring this girl to you." The look he shot Sativa was nothing short of a sneer.

Perhaps she deserved it – for how many girls would be as stupid as she had, to run away from her father's house across the sea to a man who no longer wanted her?

"What for?" a woman – presumably the queen – asked in annoyance

"I am not certain, Your Majesty, but he said something about wanting her here when he returned. Perhaps he wants you to find her a place to stay."

"Find her a room befitting her station, then," said the queen, dismissing him.

The man waited until the door was closed before he swore and turned to Sativa. "Follow me, you," he said curtly, setting off at a fast clip.

Sativa itched for a glimpse of the queen, the woman with the commanding voice that Reidar preferred over her, but she would probably see the woman at dinner. More important that she find her room first.

The man led her down several passageways, the aroma of cooking increasing in strength the further they went. Rooms above the kitchen would not be so bad, Sativa decided. She'd never miss a meal, for she'd smell it cooking.

The man stopped, then pointed through a doorway that had no door. "You'll sleep in there."

Curiously, Sativa stepped inside. At first, the

dimly lit room looked like another passageway, until her eyes adjusted and she saw that it was wider than that. Rows of straw pallets lined each side of the room, some with blankets or sacking coverlets, and others without. Pegs on the walls held an assortment of dresses and caps all made in a similar theme: practicality. If it weren't for the dresses, she'd have thought it a barracks hall, but the clothing marked it for what it was. The servants' quarters, where the castle maids slept.

On – Sativa sneezed – thrice-damned straw, the bane of her existence.

Sativa sneezed twice more before she turned on her heel and marched back the way she'd come. The man who'd guided her had disappeared, but no matter. Sativa would find her own way back to the queen's chamber, and confront the woman herself. She might be a queen, but Sativa was a princess, born with royal blood, and she would not endure such an insult.

After one wrong turning, she managed to

return to the queen's chamber, and Sativa did not bother to knock. Instead, she burst into the room.

"What is the meaning of this?" Sativa demanded in the tone she knew carried to the farthest reaches of her father's court.

"Who in heaven's name are you?" the queen countered.

For the first time, Sativa saw her, and was startled to see she recognised the woman. Oh, she was older, certainly, her fair hair almost completely white, but Regina's haughty expression had not changed a bit. This was the queen? Not Reidar's wife, but his mother?

Relief flooded through her, giving her all the authority she needed to snap, "I am Princess Sativa, daughter of King Boreslas in Kasmirus, betrothed to King Reidar of Viken, and when he returns, I will be the queen of this place. What do you think Reidar will say when he discovers you sent me to sleep with the servants?"

Regina's eyebrows rose so high, they

vanished into her hair. "Sativa? The dragon's prize girl? Impossible. She disappeared from her father's court months ago. The girl is dead."

"I am not a prize, and I am not dead," Sativa hissed through gritted teeth. "I will marry your son, and I demand the hospitality that was promised. With a bed befitting my station."

Regina managed to arrange her icy expression into a smile that held no warmth at all. "Very well, Princess. You may join me for dinner, by which time your bed will be prepared."

Sativa could afford to be gracious. "Thank you. I shall need some suitable clothing, too."

Regina eyed her tunic with the same distaste Sativa had once held for Melitta's clothing, once upon a time. "Yes, you will. My ladies will dress you."

Sativa was soon bundled into Regina's dressing room, a narrow chamber full of chests containing clothes from at least three generations of women, judging by the strange styles the ladies pulled out in their search for something suitable.

"This," one said, holding up a gown that glittered even in the dim light in the dressing room.

The gown was made of gold silk, and so richly embroidered it could probably stand up by itself. If that wasn't enough, someone had sewed dozens of jewels to it so that whoever wore it couldn't help but catch the light. It was a wedding dress, or one to be worn at a coronation. Not something for an ordinary dinner.

"It is too fine," Sativa said.

The second girl shook her head. "The queen said you must have the best. This is the richest gown in the wardrobe. If you don't wear it, the queen will punish us."

Visions of punishment aboard the *Barbe* flashed through Sativa's mind. Would Regina be so cruel as to have her ladies-in-waiting whipped? Sativa didn't want to find out.

She reached out to touch the silk. It had been so long since she'd worn anything half as pretty as this. She'd outshine everyone in the castle. Including Regina.

"Very well," Sativa said, and allowed the women to dress her.

When they were done, they guided her to the great hall, and left her with only Regina for company. Luckily, they were both at opposite ends of the great table, so she was spared the challenge of making conversation with a woman whose dislike could be felt from the other side of the room.

Sativa ate her fill of everything. It would take some time to replace the weight she'd lost aboard the *Barbe*, and she doubted Reidar wanted to introduce his people to a half-starved bride. She was a princess from a prosperous kingdom — she should look the part.

All too soon, she grew tired, and found she struggled to keep her eyes open. As Sativa tried to smother yet another yawn, Regina rose to her feet.

"My servants tell me your room is ready," Regina said. "Let me show you to your bed."

Sativa owned that it was a good idea, and followed the woman readily.

This time, the chamber wasn't far from the queen's own. A servant threw the door open and Regina peered inside. Her face lit with a genuine smile.

"Behold, Princess, a bed befitting your high station," Regina said, dropping a curtsey.

Finally. Sativa stepped into the room, expecting either another straw pallet or the sort of fine feather bed she had at home. Neither would have surprised her. What she did see made her jaw drop. It wasn't one fine feather bed, but at least a dozen, the mattresses stacked so high they nearly reached the ceiling. Sativa stopped to count them all. No, not a dozen. Twenty of the things, with a ladder beside them to help her climb to the top.

A calculated insult, or an over-the-top honour. Sativa was certain it was meant as the former, but she smiled sweetly as though it were the latter. "Why, thank you," she simpered. "Just like the one I had at home."

Regina's composure failed, and her true hatred shone through. "Liar," she spat. "You are no more a princess than the maids in the kitchen. No one sleeps in a bed like that. You will never marry my son, for he's too good for the likes of you." She slammed the door shut and Sativa heard the key turn in the lock.

Sativa was tempted to shout something after the woman, but someone had to show their better breeding, and it had best be her.

Besides, climbing a ladder into a bed that looked softer than a cloud seemed like luxury after climbing the mast every day and sleeping in a hammock on the *Barbe*.

Sativa scaled the ladder and climbed carefully onto the stacked mattresses. She sank so deep she suspected getting out might prove a challenge, but one she would tackle after a good night's sleep on what had to be the softest bed she'd ever encountered. Silently, she thanked Reidar and his mother, for this felt like pure bliss. Yes, she would show Regina, and marry Reidar just like she'd promised. And maybe, just maybe, she'd ask him for a slightly less decadent version of this bed. One that didn't require a ladder. Because she could definitely get used to comfort like this.

Until a growing tickle in her nose could not be ignored, and she sneezed. Not once, but six times in succession. And then again.

There was straw in this room. In the mattresses, she suspected, though she had no way to tell.

"Damn you, bitch," Sativa said softly, as her eyes teared up from the straw dust in the air. That was what caused it, not emotion or self-pity or any such thing.

She only had to endure it until Reidar returned, and then everything would be rosy.

Sativa sneezed. And swore. And sneezed again.

Damned rose fever.

She hoped he came home soon.

Thirty-Seven

"What are you still doing here?"

Rudolf's words jarred Reidar out of what had been a deep sleep. In a stable, judging by the smell.

"Because I distinctly recall telling you last night that we'd take care of the damage those two boats wrought when they made it through our hail of arrows. And we did, thank you. We only lost the roof of one house to fire." Rudolf glared at Reidar. "Why aren't you home with your bride, getting ready for your wedding, like you said you would?"

Reidar's mind started to work. Now he remembered coming into the stable, calling for a groom to saddle his horse, but all the men were off defending the town, so he'd had to do the job himself. And then he'd closed his eyes for just a moment…

…and woken up here, in daylight. Reidar cursed.

"I fell asleep," he admitted.

Rudolf snorted. "I can see that. You're lucky no one's come in yet. I'm not sure what the townsfolk would do if they found a snoring king in their stable."

"I do not snore," Reidar grumbled.

"One day, I will ask your lovely wife to tell me the truth. Now, get you gone and marry the girl before someone else beats you to it!" Rudolf said.

"No one commands the king," Reidar muttered as he reached for his horse's bridle.

"As the king's cousin and heir, I think I have the right to make strong suggestions that

I think the king should follow, if he's not to turn into a complete fool," Rudolf replied. "Who else will, if I do not?"

Reidar had to admit the man was right. But he didn't have to admit it aloud, though. "Mind your manners, or I will not invite you to the wedding feast," he said as he climbed atop his horse. He set off before Rudolf could reply.

"You'll have to ask the girl to marry you first!" Rudolf shouted after him.

Curse the man, but he was right.

Sativa was in his thoughts for most of the ride home. He'd have to tread carefully, for she'd evidently endured some terrible trials between her father's castle and his. A wedding would have to wait until she was willing to let him touch her without pulling out a knife to defend herself.

He'd like to find whoever had frightened her and force them to endure whatever they'd put her through. That was a cheering thought. Perhaps he'd offer to let Sativa help, or at least observe. She would want to ensure justice was served.

But that would have to wait, too. First, he wanted to see her, to ask her what had happened, and whether she was still willing to marry him. At least he knew she was safe under his roof.

He handed the reins to a groom and vaulted off his horse in the bailey, wanting nothing more than to see Sativa again when he arrived home.

"Where is the girl I brought here yesterday?" he asked a passing serving girl, but she did not know. Nor did anyone else he asked, it seemed.

How dare they mislay their future queen?

Incensed, Reidar headed for his mother's chambers. She would know where to find Sativa. Perhaps she could also explain why the girl was being kept a secret from his own servants. They would be her servants soon enough.

"Where is she?" he demanded as he strode into her apartment.

Regina set down her embroidery. "Where is who?"

"Princess Sativa." She would not hide her identity, he was certain of it. Not here.

Regina wet her lips. "You mean the girl pretending to be the dead princess."

Reidar fought to keep his temper. "No, I mean the very real, live princess I left in your care yesterday. The one who will soon be my wife." He prayed that this last part was true.

"You're a fool, my son, but most men are. Fooled by a pretty face and a tale of distress. That girl is no more highborn than any other maid in the castle. First, she had the gall to demand to wear the most valuable gown in the castle to dinner. Then she had the effrontery to demand the most outlandish bed, which she imagined was what a princess slept upon. I'll show you, if you like. Then you'll see she is playing you for a fool." Regina rose and swept out of the room.

No. His mother was wrong. Whatever she thought, he knew he'd brought the real Sativa here yesterday. No one else could know what she did.

Regina stopped outside one of the guest apartments and turned the key in the lock.

"You locked her in, like a prisoner?" Reidar demanded. He didn't want to lose his temper, but his mother was pushing him much too far.

"I could not have her wandering around the castle. Who knows what she might steal?" Regina said, then threw open the door with a flourish.

Sativa stood on the threshold, her red eyes and nose streaming. "If this is the hospitality you show to guests, I hope the devil shows you better in hell," she said. "I scarcely slept in that travesty of a bed. It was impossible, with that bloody…that bloody…pea – aachoo!" She sneezed twice more, then glared at Regina.

"But that's not possible," Regina spluttered. "No one's so refined, so sensitive, she could sense something like that through so many mattresses. Not even royalty. How could she detect such a thing through twenty mattresses?"

Pea straw, the stuff that made her sneeze, Sativa had meant to say, Reidar was certain. He peered into the room behind her and saw a strange sight. A stack of mattresses, including the straw one his father had slept on every day of his life, insisting it was far better than feathers. The old pallet had burst under the weight of the ones above, strewing straw all over the floor. It had been better for his father, perhaps. But not for Sativa.

Who had suffered even more, and it was his fault.

Reidar fell to his knees. "Forgive me, Princess. I promised to protect you, and I failed. I'd planned to ask you to marry me, and name the day of our wedding, but I find I must beg your forgiveness first, and pay a heavy penance, before I'd dare ask anything of you."

Sativa stared down at him. Once again, sizing up his soul. Reidar prayed he would not be found wanting. "A handkerchief," she said.

He felt through his pockets, and produced

one. "I'm sorry for the soot. We set fire to half a dozen ships last night."

"Thank you," she said, inclining her head. She wiped her eyes, then delicately blew her nose. "There. You asked for…things."

She swayed on her feet and Reidar caught her, rising to his feet when he realised she needed his support. She truly hadn't slept, and she was still weak from her ordeal.

"Tomorrow," she said. "Give me a bed without straw and a hot bath, and you shall have everything you ask for tomorrow."

Reidar didn't believe his ears. "What will I have tomorrow?"

Sativa slumped against him. Exhausted, poor girl. "Wedding. Forgiveness. Whatever. But I never want to see her again." She stabbed a finger at Regina.

"I will not stay here while she's polluting the place," Regina said hotly. "I shall go to live with one of your sisters until you come to your senses." She stormed off.

Reidar didn't intend to come to his senses

any time soon. Sativa drove him wild, and he had to admit he rather liked it. Reidar lifted Sativa in his arms. "Whatever you wish, my queen," he said softly.

She smiled. "A bed," she said before her eyes closed. "And don't go away this time."

He carried her limp form up to the tower room she should have been shown last night, and set her in the middle of the bed. He pulled the covers over her, not sure what else to do.

All he could do was wait and watch over her until she woke.

Which was what she wanted, so he did.

Thirty Eight

When Sativa woke, the sun was high in the sky, but she felt well rested.

Reidar stepped out of the shadows. "I brought you breakfast, but I fear it is cold now. I will send for some more. I didn't want to wake you."

He was as chivalrous as she'd always dreamed he'd be. But the time for chivalry was done. She would marry this man – this king – and she would pledge herself to him so irrevocably that he would truly know she meant what she said. Reidar was everything she wanted in a man, and despite what she'd said in the forest, in her heart, she belonged to him and him alone. It was time he knew that.

"Come here," Sativa said, her voice a little shaky. She'd never seduced a man before, and she was sure her inexperience showed. When Reidar turned to face her, she pulled her shift over her head and threw it on the floor, so she sat naked on the bed.

His eyes raked her body before returning to her face. "Princess…" Lust smouldered, just as it had in the forest.

She patted the bed. "Here, Reidar. My name is Sativa, not Princess. You will need to remember that, when I am your wife."

He took one tentative step closer, then another. His eyes held something akin to awe. Another step. He stopped beside the bed, as though something held him back. "Sativa." It sounded like a prayer.

"Take your clothes off, too," she said, her voice shaking even more. "I wish to see the man who will be my husband."

To her delight, he shucked off his tunic. The hard muscles she'd held onto during their ride here were everything she'd imagined. Arms, chest, back…everything.

She rose up onto her knees, reaching out to touch.

He took a step back. "Don't," he begged. "If you touch me, I'm not sure I'll be able to restrain myself. I want you, the way a man wants his wife."

Looking down, Sativa saw that what he said was true. And she wanted him, too.

"Show me everything," she said, her voice breathless. "Take all your clothes off."

His eyes burned into hers as he did as she asked. Shoes, hose, until he stood as naked as she.

Then she rose from the bed, her steps as tentative as his had been before. She forced herself to stop when she was only a step away so she could gaze at his body before she said, "What a glorious husband you will make." She swallowed, then added, "I want you the way a woman wants a lover."

Then she pressed her body against his, softness moulding around hardness, and lifted her lips for a kiss. His arm was firm at her back as his other hand cupped her cheek. No more words were necessary for his eyes said it all as he kissed her, tenderly at first then with an urgency that rivalled her own. Long and deep and so delicious he made her dizzy.

"I have dreamed of this," she gasped.

"So have I," he said. "Tomorrow, after we are wed – "

"No," she interrupted. "I don't want to wait. I want you now." She reached down and wrapped her hand around his manhood. So hard, and yet so soft. What would it feel like inside her?

Gently, he pried her hand loose. "Sativa." Another prayer, as her fingers stroked his length before she let go.

Her eyes met his. "Show me how you will love your queen." Taking his hand, she led him to the bed, then lay down.

Something warred in his eyes. Sativa didn't care what, as long as she won.

"You said you would take me as your queen. So, take me."

He smiled. "As my queen commands." He climbed onto the bed beside her, his hands brushing lightly over her skin so that she shivered. His smile broadened, before he covered her body in kisses. She gasped and sighed under his caresses, until he said, "Sativa, have you ever taken a lover before?"

She sat up in surprise. "Of course not. I've been promised to you since I was six!"

He chuckled. "That never stopped the ladies of Viken from taking lovers if they liked. Marriage means being faithful to only the one. But if I am your first…then I must make sure you are prepared for me."

His caresses and kisses grew more fervent, making her gasp with delight as he drew pleasure from her body that she had not thought possible. After an eternity of foreplay, finally he declared that she was ready.

Sativa opened her mouth to say that she had been ready long before, but the sensation of him entering her took her breath away. She opened her legs wider, welcoming him inside. That first thrust seemed to take a glorious eternity, until she could take no more, for he had filled her completely.

She closed her eyes, relishing the pure pleasure she had never before imagined.

Reidar leaned forward, pushing deliciously deeper into her as he cupped her face in gentle hands. "Sativa, please tell me if I am too much for you. I will stop, I swear."

She opened her eyes, smiling in joy. "Don't stop, my king. Don't stop until we are both spent, and need to rest, before we can make love some more." At this, he moved within her and she moaned in pleasure. "Yes, more!"

Their bodies melded together in a union so perfect Sativa could not have dreamed it before this moment, and this moment was one she never wanted to end. A moment of unfathomable bliss between two shared souls. A promise joyfully fulfilled.

Much later, when the sunset light streamed through the window and kissed their naked bodies, lying side by side on the bed, Reidar turned to her and said, "Tomorrow is our wedding. After today, what will I have left to give you on our wedding night?"

Sativa laughed softly. "More of the same, I imagine, unless you have a different kind of lovemaking in mind. If we do this enough, we are sure to have a child. But until we do, give me the gift of your body, and your love, and I shall give you mine in return. Every day and every night, so that we may live happily ever after."

About the Author

Demelza Carlton has always loved the ocean, but on her first snorkelling trip she found she was afraid of fish.

She has since swum with sea lions, sharks and sea cucumbers and stood on spray drenched cliffs over a seething sea as a seven-metre cyclonic swell surged in, shattering a shipwreck below.

Demelza now lives in Perth, Western Australia, the shark attack capital of the world.

The *Ocean's Gift* series was her first foray into fiction, followed by her suspense thriller *Nightmares* trilogy. She swears the *Mel Goes to Hell* series ambushed her on a crowded train and wouldn't leave her alone.

Want to know more? You can follow Demelza on Facebook, Twitter, YouTube or her website, Demelza Carlton's Place at:

www.demelzacarlton.com

Books by Demelza Carlton

Ocean's Gift series

Ocean's Gift (#1)
Ocean's Infiltrator (#2)
Ocean's Depths (#3)
Water and Fire

Turbulence and Triumph series

Ocean's Justice (#1)
Ocean's Trial (#2)
Ocean's Triumph (#3)
Ocean's Ride (#4)
Ocean's Cage (#5)
Ocean's Birth (#6)
How To Catch Crabs

Nightmares Trilogy

Nightmares of Caitlin Lockyer (#1)
Necessary Evil of Nathan Miller (#2)
Afterlife of Alana Miller (#3)

Mel Goes to Hell series

Welcome to Hell (#1)
See You in Hell (#2)
Mel Goes to Hell (#3)
To Hell and Back (#4)
The Holiday From Hell (#5)
All Hell Breaks Loose (#6)

Romance Island Resort series

Maid for the Rock Star (#1)
The Rock Star's Email Order Bride (#2)
The Rock Star's Virginity (#3)
The Rock Star and the Billionaire (#4)
The Rock Star Wants A Wife (#5)
The Rock Star's Wedding (#6)
Maid for the South Pole (#7)
Jailbird Bride (#8)

The Complex series

Halcyon
Fishtail